THE WOMAN I BEFRIENDED

By Sara Kate

As always, this book is dedicated to my husband and my father.

THE WOMAN I BEFRIENDED

JULY

1

I think a serial killer lives in the house across the street from me. Out of all my neighbors, she is the only person I don't know.

Okay, I don't know any of my neighbors *personally*, but I know enough about them. That is, except for the woman across the street.

I've noticed she has a weird sense of style. Whether it is daytime or night, I usually see her dressed in black pants and an oversized T-shirt, or sweatpants and a hoodie.

We live in North Florida. Sweatpants and hoodies are normally only acceptable in the winter. Not during the summer, as we just entered the first week of July.

I saw her wearing a blue sweatshirt with matching sweatpants just two nights ago when she was leaving her house.

It was nearly ninety degrees outside.

Besides my neighbor's peculiar choice of clothing in the Florida weather, her routine is strange too.

She leaves her house just before midnight three nights a week: Tuesday, Wednesday, and Thursday. She doesn't come home until after five o'clock in the morning the next day.

On Fridays and Sundays, she's out of her house by eight-thirty in the morning and comes home at six o'clock in the evening.

And the most mysterious thing that I have noticed about my neighbor of all: men have gone into her house on different occasions, but I have never seen anyone come out.

Sure, a woman who brings home a guy for a one-night stand is not unheard of.

But none of her one-night stands leave her house the next day; like last night and this morning.

Through the blinds on my double-hung windows in my living room, I watched my neighbor pull her Jeep into her driveway late last night. She stepped out of the driver's side while a guy, who I've never seen before, got out of the passenger side. He followed her right into her house.

After I woke up this morning, I checked my security camera that is mounted on my front porch to see if he left yet, but there was no recording of him leaving.

My camera isn't angled to view my neighbor's front door, but it does see her driveway and the street that is between our houses. It's also set up to record motion, so it normally catches any movement outside; including when cars drive by and when people walk on the road.

I know my camera would have recorded if that man called a ride and got picked up between last night and this morning, and it hasn't yet.

He's still in there.

Last night was not the first time I noticed this behavior of my neighbor.

About three weeks ago, I saw her bring home a different guy. When I played back the footage from my camera the next morning, I saw her leave in her Jeep without him. Since I knew she wasn't home at the time, I walked over and knocked on her front door, hoping the guy would open the door. But when nobody answered, I walked around to her backyard which is conveniently not fenced in.

Also convenient, her sliding back door was left unlocked too. Even though I wanted to, I did not walk inside her house. I only slid the door open and called out to see if the guy was still there, but I never got a response. I didn't see him in the living room from where I was standing outside and there was no sign of anyone in the house at the time either.

There also weren't any dead bodies or incriminating evidence just lying around out in the woman's home either.

But that obviously does not make me rule the woman out as a killer yet. Especially now, since there is a new guy in her house that hasn't come out yet.

And I still haven't figured out where the last guy went. I also now regret not walking in her house. Maybe the guy was lying dead in her bedroom when I poked my head through the doorway.

Something is strange about her. I feel it.

Ding. The coffee startles me when it finishes brewing in the kitchen. I divert my attention away from the front window.

"Coffee's ready," I call out to my husband, Noah who is getting ready for work in our bedroom down the hallway from our kitchen.

During the weekdays, Noah leaves to go to the office at around eight in the morning and I'm in my desk chair in our living room by ten o'clock. Sometimes, eleven o'clock if I open a bottle of wine after my coffee which I might do today.

Since it's Sunday, neither Noah and I are scheduled to work but he chose to go into the office today because he needs to prepare for a few upcoming campaigns that he is working on.

Since I have no life, I'll work for a few hours this morning to make the day go by.

A perk about working from home: you can pick up shifts whenever you want.

You can also drink as much wine as you want.

"Morning." Noah greets me when he sees the plate of eggs and coffee that I left on our small two-seater black table for him.

"Morning," I sit across from him. "Have you noticed our neighbor across the street?"

Noah takes a bite of his eggs, giving me a bizarre look. "What about her?"

"Have you noticed her?" I repeat.

"I noticed she lives there." He tilts his head, curious.

I never ask my husband about other women.

"She seems weird." I shrug.

"I think you should introduce yourself to her.

"Make a friend," he suggests, innocently and oblivious to how difficult making friends has become for me lately.

"I don't know if I want to be her friend." I sip my coffee. "I have a strange feeling about her. She leaves late at night a few times during the week... I wonder where she goes."

"Maybe she's going to work. She probably works an overnight shift somewhere," Noah mumbles in between chews.

"I don't know what job requires a person to wear sweatpants and large T-shirts." I make a face of contemplation. "And hoodies..."

Shrugging, Noah doesn't question my comment about the woman's wardrobe and continues eating his food. I doubt he's ever noticed what the woman wears or what she even looks like.

Well, I don't really know what she looks like either. I have never seen her face up close, but I think she's pretty. From afar, I have noticed that she has curly brunette hair. She normally styles it in a ponytail that falls just a bit past her shoulders.

Unlike me, it doesn't look like she wears a lot of makeup because her complexion appears clear. If she does wear makeup, then she applies her foundation very well.

And she also looks like she could be around my age; thirty or possibly in her late twenties.

"Maybe she's got a boyfriend. She probably sleeps over at his house." Noah follows my gaze toward the window in our living room. "Or girlfriend."

"I don't think so because I've seen different men go into her house." I shake my head.

"Okay, so maybe she's a hooker." Noah laughs.

"I doubt that." I scrunch my forehead. "She has to be single. There's a man in her house right now. I saw him get out of her Jeep last night."

"Maybe she's cheating on someone." Noah huffs with a mouthful of food.

I shake my head again, doubtfully.

"Stop stalking the neighbors, babe." Noah smiles.

"It's not my fault we have a beautiful window that I get to sit in front of all day." I roll my eyes, grinning.

"You wanted your desk there," he smirks.

To be fair, Noah's right. I chose to put my desk in front of the window in our living room when I got hired as a bill collection agent two years ago. I wanted natural light in the room besides a bright monitor screen in front of my face all day.

Before two years ago, however, I never had an interest in watching my neighbors because I was never home. A nine-to-five job in an office as a receptionist took most of my late-twenties away and I hated it. I hate being a collection agent too, but I prefer the flexible schedule and the fact that I can drink wine and be home all day.

I hadn't realized placing my desk in front of the window would inadvertently cause me to watch my neighbors, but so be it.

You should know who is living in your neighborhood. I happen to think we might be living across the street from a serial killer.

As neighbors, we should probably know that.

"Why are you suddenly so interested in this

woman?" Noah asks.

"I don't know. I get curious. You know that." I sigh.

"Oh, I know you do." Noah raises his eyebrows.

Oh yes, I know he knows.

We both do and we both don't need a reminder which is why I will not share my true thoughts about our neighbor with my husband just yet. Noah believes in me about ninety-nine percent of most things.

However, if I bring up the thought of a serial killer living across from us, much less a killer living in our neighborhood at all, he may want me to go see my therapist again.

And it is not that serious this time. I don't need to talk to a therapist about this.

"That's why I think you should introduce yourself. Next time you see her outside, you should wave." Noah smiles and I know he is right.

It hasn't been so easy for me to socialize since my best friend, Laura, who was also my only friend, died two years ago.

I'm also never faced with many opportunities to just *make a friend,* as my husband so kindly just suggested.

"Sorry I have to work this weekend. I think I'm going to put in for some vacation days once I'm done traveling. I need a break," he says as he stands up from the table.

"I understand, babe." I agree even though I don't understand at all because I have never been under any sort of pressure from a job like my husband has been under.

Noah has worked in marketing for ten years; the entire time we've been together. It wasn't until four years ago when he got promoted to marketing director which has come with a lot of traveling. His job is the only thing we don't have in common together.

When I am saying goodbye to my husband at the front door, my eyes drift across the street toward our neighbor's house. Noah turns around and looks in the same direction.

The woman is taking her trash down to the garbage can at the end of her driveway. She's wearing black pants like I usually see her wear, but surprisingly…a white tank top. Not a large T-shirt or hoodie.

"Now's your chance." Noah pushes a brunette strand of my hair behind my ear, then kisses me and I wish him a good day at work.

Make a friend. I know my husband is trying to be helpful, but it is not so easy to just walk up to another woman and ask to be her friend. Even when Laura was alive, I never socialized with anyone else besides her and my husband.

Lately, the only conversations that I take part in are with customers when taking payments on the phone and small talk with the cashier at the grocery store or coffee shop. I don't even have a hobby.

Well, besides watching my neighbors. Although, I am not sure that's my hobby. I think that is more of an added perk to working from home.

But maybe I should take Noah's suggestion this morning. Maybe, I'll make a friend. And maybe it will be with a serial killer.

2

Noah's suggestion sounded good. Although, I think my idea is much better.

I just walked out of my front door with a bag of trash that my husband forgot to take out before he left for work this morning. On a regular day, his forgetfulness would slightly irritate me. Except not today.

Today, the trash is a good excuse to knock on my neighbor's door.

After I throw out my trash in the garbage can at the end of my driveway, I cross the street to walk up the driveway of my neighbor's house.

A moment after knocking on her gray front door, the door opens only about a foot wide, and I finally see her face up close for the first time.

Just like I thought, she *is* pretty.

Unlike the ponytail that I usually see her hair styled in, beautiful voluminous brunette curls fall just an inch past her shoulders. Her hair length and color are identical to mine, except my hair weighs a lot less than hers. Mine is not as curly either.

Barely any foundation covers the woman's face; that is if she is wearing any at all, while a light shade of mauve-colored lipstick highlights her lips. She is still dressed in a white tank top and black jeans that I saw her wearing only a few minutes ago when I was saying goodbye to Noah at the door.

"Hello…" She greets me cautiously from behind her door. Her hazel eyes look past my shoulder, toward the street behind me.

"Hi." I fake a smile. "Sorry to bother you, but would you mind if I use your cell phone? I locked myself out of my house when I was taking out the trash." I turn around to point across the street. "I live at that brown house over there. I have to call my husband so he can come back from work and let me in. Oh, my name's Ellie by the way. Sorry." I reach my hand out toward her. "It's been a hectic morning. I'm a little flustered."

"Oh, nice to meet you. I'm Chloe." She opens the door further to return my handshake. Then she pulls her cell phone out from her back pocket.

Instead of dialing Noah's number, I call my cellphone which I purposely left in my living room at home.

A few rings pass by before I hear my voice on the other end of the phone: *It's Ellie. Leave me a message and I might get back to you.*

As I end the call, Chloe tilts her head. "No answer?"

"He must be in a meeting already." I sigh, handing the phone back to her. "I'll just wait for him to come home on his lunch break later. Thanks anyway." I go to turn away, but Chloe calls me back over.

"Wait, I was just getting ready for work, but…" She looks back into her house. "You can wait here while I get ready. Try calling your husband again in a few minutes if you want. It's nearly a hundred degrees outside. You'll sweat to death out there."

I wasn't expecting her to invite me in but this works too.

Thanking Chloe, I walk inside where I step right into a living room decorated with light blue walls and a beige sofa.

To my left, is her yellow and blue tropical themed kitchen.

The sliding glass door that leads out to her backyard which she doesn't know I slid open before is right behind her couch. A hallway leads out from the living room on my right where I assume I would find a bedroom and a bathroom, but I can't see that far down the hall from where I stand.

And there is no guy here either. Neither is there any sign of a male ever being in this house.

No video games or controllers anywhere. No male clothes lying around. No shoes that are in men's style or sizes by the door.

Maybe the guy who I saw get out of her Jeep last night is still sleeping in her bedroom down the hallway.

Or maybe he's already dead.

"Make yourself comfortable." Chloe gestures toward the couch for me to sit. "There's soda in the fridge and bottled water if you want something to drink," she offers before disappearing into the hallway.

I step into her kitchen, except not for a drink that she offered me.

Her blue leather purse is sitting on the counter, unzipped and wide open, next to the kitchen sink.

I know I shouldn't, but I can't stop myself. My curiosity is setting in. Her wallet is sitting right there in the middle of her purse. I can see it.

My hands move before my brain makes the right decision.

Her license is suddenly in the palm of my right hand.

Chloe Jones. Height: 5'6. Age: thirty years old.

She's just a couple months older than me. Her address is even updated to this house address already.

I find that a little surprising since she just moved here earlier this year. Don't people normally procrastinate on that sort of thing?

I guess I wouldn't know. I've lived in my house for nine years.

Oh... shit. Where did all this come from?

Underneath Chloe's wallet, I pick up a plastic zip-lock bag full of singles, fives, and ten-dollar bills.

So maybe my husband was right.

Maybe she is a hooker.

Or a stripper.

Why else have all this cash in a zip lock bag?

Is that where she goes when she leaves late at night during the week? To the strip club?

In baggy clothing though?

"Want to try calling again?" Chloe's voice startles me as I hear a door open from the hallway.

Fumbling, I zip the wallet in her purse before I back away from the counter.

Chloe walks into the living room, still wearing black pants. Although instead of the white tank-top that she had on only a few minutes ago, she changed into a black collared T-shirt that I have never seen her wear until now. *Jack's Market* decorates the front of the shirt.

I have also never seen her at the grocery store when I do my shopping. Jack's Market is right down the road from here and I have been shopping at that store for years now.

Using Chloe's phone, I dial my own number again.

A couple of rings later, after I hear my own voicemail, I hang up. "No luck."

"Damn, well I got to get to work..." Chloe makes a face like she wishes she could help me more.

I am not sure that I believe her.

"It's okay. Thanks anyways."

"Want to text him at least?" she asks before putting her phone in her purse.

I am about to say yes until I remember that I would be texting my own phone number.

Chloe should not learn my number this way.

Actually, I should probably delete it out of her phone history. Just to be safe.

"No. I'll just call again, and I'll leave a voicemail this time," I say, and she hands me her phone.

After dialing my number again and hearing myself tell me to leave a voicemail, I begin.

"Hey babe, I locked myself out of the house when I was taking out the trash just now. Can you come home to let me in? This is the neighbor's cell. She's going to work soon so don't call or text back. I'll just wait outside the house. Love you."

As I am ending the call and deleting my number in her call history, I see Chloe throw on an oversized plain black T-shirt over her *Jack's Market* uniform.

"Why do you cover your work shirt like that?" I blurt out.

"Excuse me?" She shoots me a taken aback look when styling her hair into the ponytail I normally see her hair styled in.

"Well… like you said, it's basically a hundred degrees out. Isn't that hot to drive in? Two shirts?" I shift my feet, shrugging.

"Good point." Chloe laughs. "You're right. It's kind of hot to drive in, but I don't want one of our neighbors to know where I work. Jeff, the guy who lives two houses down in the apartment complex…" She gestures toward her front door, and I know exactly who she is talking about. "Well, we had a thing after I moved in and he became a little, slightly obsessive over me for a while."

I know. I saw him knock on your door several times for about two months after you moved in.

It was obvious that Chloe and Jeff were dating but not for long. I just figured whatever they had going on ended quickly and Jeff got a little too attached. He did seem obsessive, although I haven't seen him near Chloe's house in a while now. I barely ever even see him outside. He leaves for work early mornings just before sunrise and comes back home around nine o'clock at night. He's a construction worker during the week, and on the weekends, he works at his family's restaurant. The man is hardly home.

See, I know about my neighbors.

"I shop at Jack's Market all the time. I'm surprised I never noticed you there."

"Oh, that's probably because I work at the Jack's Market that's on the other side of town. Not the one that's located down the street." She shakes her head. "I don't like the manager at the store over here."

"I see." I nod, suppressing the urge to ask why.

So, Chloe covers her work shirt with baggy shirts and sweatshirts because she doesn't want Jeff to see her work shirt. Maybe she is worried that he will show up at the store and harass her. That reason seems plausible, although I don't think Jeff would go *that* far.

Then again, I don't really know the man besides his working schedule and name. He looks harmless, but sometimes harmless looking people can be the most dangerous.

Just like Chloe. She looks harmless, but I also think she could be capable of several murders.

I'm just not sure how yet.

Unless Jeff is not Chloe's real reason for covering up her work shirt and she's using him as an excuse to lie to me because she is a murderer, and my instincts about her are right.

Chloe could be hiding her place of work, so nobody sees where she's finding her victims to take back home and kill.

Is she finding them at Jack's Market?

That would be an unusual place to find your victims… unusually smart.

Or maybe Chloe finds her victims at the strip club because that wad of cash in her purse is not from receiving tips for working as a cashier in a grocery store.

She probably chooses the rude customers as her victims; the people who she thinks deserve it. She seems nice, so maybe she's a vigilante/ revenge/justice type killer?

Unless those kinds of killers are only in the movies.

I am not sure that I should justify it that way if I am right about all of this.

"You okay?" Chloe asks and I realize I have not said anything for a little too long that it is beginning to feel awkward.

"I get it." I smile, nodding sympathetically. "Well, your secret is safe with me."

After I walk across the street to my house, I watch Chloe's Jeep back out of her driveway and take a left down the road to drive out of our neighborhood. When she is no longer in my sight, I pull my keys out of my jean pocket to unlock my front door.

My husband will be so thrilled to hear that I took his suggestion today. Whether Chloe is a serial killer or not, I think I made a new friend this morning.

I will just make sure to leave that part out when I tell him.

3

I normally drink a few glasses of wine throughout my workday because I dread calling my customers. However, this morning after leaving Chloe's house, I poured myself a glass because I feel good.

It's exciting to make a new friend.

Maybe Chloe isn't a killer and my mind has gone a little too far.

It wouldn't be the first time I have exaggerated anything before.

As I am logging into my work portal at my desk, I stare at Chloe's now empty driveway through my window. We both left her house only half an hour ago.

I just played back my security footage from my front porch again to see if I missed a recording of when the man left Chloe's house earlier, but I didn't miss anything.

But I was just inside her house myself, so where was he?

There is no way he left through her backyard because there isn't a road behind Chloe's house. Her backyard leads right out to one of two large forests in this town.

So where is he now?

I was just in her house, and I am about ninety-nine percent sure he wasn't there.

I need to knock on her door again.

Maybe he was sleeping in her bedroom when I was there and now, hopefully he's awake.

Or maybe I will find him dead in her bedroom.

There is no way that I can focus on work right now anyway.

Instead of calling my first customer, I leave my house to walk across the street.

When I arrive at Chloe's front door, I knock on the gray-painted wood twice.

No answer. Guess I will have to go through the backyard like I did a few weeks ago.

Thankfully the neighbors on both sides of her house are already at work so nobody should notice me walk back here.

Unlike the last time I did this, Chloe's sliding door is locked today.

I press my face against the semi-tinted glass. Nobody is inside her living room or in the kitchen.

"Hello?" I knock on the glass door.

No answer.

"Hello?" I call out again. "Anyone there?"

If that man is still in this house, then he is either purposely ignoring me, he's still sleeping and can't hear me, or he's dead.

I guess I won't find out because I am not about to break into this woman's house right now. If only her back door was unlocked again. This time, I would walk in.

I also need to get back to work. Or start working, I should say.

As I am walking back toward the front of Chloe's house, across the street, I spot the front door start to open on the house that is on the right of mine.

Shit. The time on my phone tells me it's ten o'clock: *Time for my next-door neighbor's daily morning run.* She should not see me walking back from Chloe's house without Chloe.

That would look strange.

So, I wait a moment, remaining in the backyard near the side of Chloe's house. After I watch my neighbor run down her driveway and down the road, I continue to head home.

But as I am walking up my driveway, my phone buzzes with an unusual sound that I can't remember the last time hearing.

AMBER ALERT.
Missing Child. Chuck County.
Avery, Florida.

I go to swipe the alert off my screen, but I accidentally click on the notification instead.

It brings me to a missing persons report with a picture of a teenage girl. Besides her photo, the description reads:

A Florida Amber Alert has been issued for Bianca Ramirez. 14-years-old. Height: 5'0. Last seen with her friends getting off the bus at the bus stop, but never made it to her home in Avery, Florida. Chuck County.

The last time I heard of someone going missing around here was about two years ago, only two months after Laura died.

But I never got an Amber Alert about the missing woman who was named Jenna at that time. I heard about her disappearance on the news. Jenna's sister said she never came home from a late-night work shift. She was only twenty-four years old when she went missing.

To this day, two years later, Jenna has never been found.

I walk into my house and go to my desk. Out of curiosity and procrastination in starting work, I Google *missing persons in Avery, Florida.*

I know I shouldn't be doing this.

But the Amber Alert has me curious.

The first website that is shown in the search results connects to the online missing persons database for Avery, Florida.

And to my surprise, thirteen results show up.

Avery is not considered a small town, but it is relatively small enough with a population of around twenty-thousand people.

We only have one police station here and a substation.

I don't get it. How could so many people be listed missing? I'd expect maybe three or four but not thirteen.

My eyes scan through the most recent disappearances underneath Bianca who is the first reported missing person on the list.

Devon Gomes. Age 31. 5'9. Reported missing on June 17th. Last seen getting drinks at a bar downtown with a friend.

Albert George. Age 72. 5'8. Reported missing by his daughter on May 2nd. Family reports he has dementia. He went missing after leaving the house to go for a walk in his neighborhood around noon.

Ryan Davis. Age 25. 5'9. Reported missing on May 12th by his sister.

Valeria Lopez. Age 17. 5'2. Reported on May 20th as a runaway teenager.

Theo Dian. Age 29. 6'0. Reported missing on April 19th by his mother after not hearing from him.

The rest of the seven disappearances on this list date back to last year and a few years before then:

Two teenagers were reported missing last year while a third teenager went missing three years ago.

Two women, one in her thirties, the other in her twenties; both with a history of drug abuse were reported missing four years ago.

Five years ago, a man in his fifties was last seen before going fishing. His boat was found without him in it.

And lastly, Jenna; the woman who made the news two years ago is on this list.

Besides Jenna, I am sure I've seen one, if not all of the teenagers on the news, but I know I haven't seen or heard about everyone else on this list until now.

A statement below Jenna's photo, along with each person that has been missing for any time over a year says: **At Avery Police Station, we never stop searching for missing persons.**

Scrolling back up to the top of the list, I focus on the disappearances from this year only.

Besides the two teenagers: Bianca and Valeria, I notice the rest of the four people that have disappeared within this year, specifically within these past few months… are all males.

But I also notice something else.

Besides Albert, the elderly man with dementia, the other three men are all in their mid to late twenties.

And they're all tall, over five foot nine.

That could be a coincidence…

But still… I have never heard of an adult male reported as missing without reason. Especially three of them within a year… in this town.

It's always children or women that make the news stories and the amber alerts.

But of course, adult men go missing. Just like females, men can be victims too.

This list proves it.

4

J u l y   1 0 t h   F r i d a y

A week went by, and I didn't speak to Chloe until she knocked on my door yesterday morning with two iced coffees in her hands.

She only brought me a coffee because the barista made her drink wrong the first time. So he let her keep it, along with the correct drink. Chloe didn't have anyone to give the coffee to, so she brought it to me.

I invited her inside of my house which is something I never do but it felt like the appropriate response as a thank you for the drink. She only stayed in my house for a few minutes, admiring my burgundy red walls in my living room and the beautiful double-hung windows by my desk that she has no clue I watch her through.

Just like how I watched her through them this morning. I saw Chloe leave her house at eight-thirty wearing black pants and an oversized shirt as usual.

I assume she is going to work at Jack's since the black pants are a part of her uniform.

At night, she usually wears sweatpants, probably covering whatever lingerie she has underneath them.

That sounds a little backwards to me, stripping or hooking during the weekday nights and working at a grocery store on the weekend.

But then again, I am only assuming so far.

There is no need for me to drive to the Jack's Market location where Chloe works to do my grocery shopping. However, I took the drive to her store today. With traffic, Jack's is about a ten-minute drive from my house.

Today is my day off work and as usual, I have no plans. My fridge is on the verge of being empty and I wanted to stay out of the house longer since Noah is working overtime today.

A lot of preparation that I don't really understand goes into marketing campaigns. The last three out of town campaigns are scheduled throughout the next few months.

As for the specific one that he is currently working on, I can't even begin to explain, even though Noah has described it in detail to me many times. Work and I are in two different worlds of my husbands.

Since Noah won't be home until tonight, I thought it would be a good idea to visit my new friend, Chloe and get my grocery shopping done all at once.

I have not entirely ruled out if she is a killer or no but if not, then I think we could be friends. We kind of already are. I mean, she brought me coffee. If I was her first choice of person to bring a free coffee to, that tells me she doesn't have many friends. If she has any at all.

Thinking about it now, for such a friendly woman who invites me; a total stranger inside her home, I wouldn't expect her to not have any friends though. She was hesitant to answer the door until she realized I needed help. Then she became friendlier.

In that logic, then I guess I should not suspect her as a killer either.

A killer would not willingly invite a stranger in their house.

Actually… yes.

A killer likely *would* do that…

After walking through the entrance of Jack's Market, it takes only about two minutes before I spot Chloe standing behind one of the registers. She is ringing up an elderly lady's groceries who just pulled a handful of coupons out of her purse. Chloe doesn't seem to mind even though the line of people waiting to checkout is starting to get longer. The customer right behind the elderly woman is visibly aggravated, tapping his hands on the railing of his shopping cart and rolling his eyes, sighing loudly.

I watch Chloe wait patiently as the woman finishes the transaction with a bag of coins and a few dollar bills. Then Chloe goes on to deal with the next customer, the already aggravated idiot. She's calm and smiling like how she handled the elderly woman.

Chloe doesn't even seem fazed that he's tapping his fingers impatiently on the credit card machine. When the receipt prints out of the register, he snatches it before Chloe gets the chance to grab it herself and hand to him. Still, Chloe remains quiet and moves on to the next customer, unbothered by his crudeness.

If that were me, I would have told that guy to fuck off.

As I watch Chloe interact with her customers, she doesn't really seem or look like a killer, but then again, the Golden State Killer didn't look like a murderer either.

If a seventy-year-old man who has an entire family can get away with several murders for over a decade, then a single thirty-year-old woman can probably get away with murder too, right?

Hell, she would probably get away with it easier.

If my instincts are correct, I should play it safe. I can't let Chloe know that I am suspicious of her. Coming to the grocery store was a mistake of mine.

Instead of going to her register to ring up my groceries after I am done with my shopping, I will choose self-checkout.

5

"I'm really glad that hurricane isn't going to come this way," Chloe says as she looks at the trees swaying in the woods behind her backyard.

I throw my hair up into a quick messy bun on top of my head. "The wind feels nice though."

During small talk at my mailbox with Chloe this morning, I mentioned I wanted to try a new take-out restaurant that just opened down the street from us. Chloe told me she wanted to try the same place, so she invited me over for dinner.

Now here we are, sitting in her backyard next to each other in two ocean blue colored recliner chairs, facing the woods behind her yard. She picked up the burgers on the way home from Jack's and I brought a bottle of wine over.

See, I knew we were becoming friends.

"You really like the beach, don't you?" I question, touching the blue cloth on the chair.

Her kitchen and living room are draped in beachy décor just like this chair. I haven't seen her bedroom, but I am sure it is decked out in ocean blue as well.

Or decked out in blood… from her victims.
Blood splattered on the ocean blue walls…

"I just like a tropical vibe throughout my house. It brings me peace," Chloe answers.

"Makes sense." I straighten up. "So, I haven't gone out in a while…" I set my drink down on the deck floor next to my seat. For such a nice backyard, I would use it more than Chloe does.

I would at least own a table to put my food and drinks on.

"I was thinking about going out to a bar this Tuesday night. Want to come with me? Noah has to work late. He's been preparing for a campaign that he's traveling out of town for at the end of the month," I shrug. "I don't know. I've just been wanting to get out of the house lately."

I am not thinking about going to a bar or socializing anywhere. I am just trying to see what Chloe's response will be because she leaves her house just before midnight on Tuesdays. If she's a stripper, then this would be the time to tell me.

"I wish." Chloe sips the last of her wine. "I work Tuesday nights."

"Oh, at Jack's?" I laugh, scrunching my forehead.

She leans over to grab the wine bottle off the floor in the middle of our chairs and pours herself another glass. "No. I'm a cocktail waitress at the

Ghost Go-Go bar downtown. I work there a couple of nights during the week. I'm at Jack's all day on Fridays and Sundays. Sometimes Saturdays too, if I want the extra money. Like tomorrow, I picked up an extra shift."

"Oh!" I say with more enthusiasm in my voice than I intended to let out.

Chloe's not a stripper but she works with women who dance half-naked on top of a bar. My assumption was close enough.

"Why do you sound… surprised?" Chloe asks, curiosity in her voice.

"I, uh, I thought you were a stripper," I admit, thinking back to the zip-lock bag full of bills in her purse. That was probably her tip money from waitressing.

I guess that makes sense.

"Oh, hell no!" Chloe laughs. "I don't have that much confidence in myself." She narrows her eyes. "Wait, why did you think that of me?"

"Oh, I just noticed that you leave late at night sometimes. I figured you had a second job. I don't know." I shift my body to get more comfortable. "If you haven't noticed, I can be a bit of a bored housewife. Well, not really a housewife, I guess…" I let my words linger. "I do have a job."

"You do?" Chloe sits up.

"Don't judge me, but I'm a bill collector."

Nobody likes bill collectors.

"Hey, I'm not judging!" Chloe shakes her head, smiling. "I literally serve drunk people for a living. Whatever brings in money, right?"

I nod. "My job is really to keep me busy. I could probably do something else for work, but I don't really want to…" As the words leave my mouth, I realize that I really don't need my job anymore.

Noah's income sustains the both of us. I only started working as a collection agent after getting extremely fed up with my receptionist job one day and impulsively quitting. After being humiliated by a customer because I made a mistake with the schedule, I walked out of the office and never went back. I spent the next two weeks searching for online jobs and applied to anything that allowed me to work from home, even if I didn't have any experience that the job required. Which was the case for nearly everything I applied to.

When the collection agency called me first, I took the position right away. After hearing, 'work from home', 'Make your own schedule' and 'wouldn't have to sell anything,' I was sold.

"I get it. You're complacent." Chloe's comment surprises me.

Complacent? I didn't think I was… complacent.

"I guess. So, you live in this house alone? It's nice." I turn my head to look toward the sliding glass door behind us.

This house is a little too nice for a thirty-year-old single woman, in my opinion. The house isn't large but is of a decent size. A one bed and one bath.

This backyard is nice too. It's just big enough to put an above ground pool back here and still have space for these chairs.

And also a table.

"This house is the reason I have two jobs," Chloe sighs. "I stupidly thought my ex-boyfriend would stick to his word and pay his portion of the rent that we *both* agreed with, when we first moved in, but I was wrong. He didn't last more than two weeks here with me before I kicked his ass out."

What a liar.

"His loss." I give a supportive grin. "Any new guy in your life now?"

"Nope and not for a while!" Chloe sips her drink. "What's that phrase? Let nature run its course… or let time fall into place?" She shrugs. "I'm not looking to get in a relationship right now. I need some time for myself."

"I get it." I nod, but of course I don't get it at all.

I check the time on my phone because Noah should be home from work in a few minutes.

Chloe notices. "Husband on the way home?"

"How'd you know that?" I look up from my cell phone with creased eyebrows.

"You said it yourself. You're a housewife. What else would you be checking the time for?" She gives me a *'what else in your life is important?'* look.

I admit, she's kind of right.

"He works a lot, doesn't he?" Chloe asks.

"What?" I look at her, confused.

"Your husband. He works a lot, huh?"

Why is she asking me about my husband?

I don't think I like her tone of voice. She sounds skeptical of him.

"Yeah, full-time," I nod.

"Office guy, huh?" She shakes her head.

I nod again.

"Doesn't that ever worry you?"

"What do you mean?"

"Well, I'm sure he's around other women a lot in the office, right?" Chloe tilts her head. "He probably meets a lot of people when he travels."

"I don't know. I've never been to his office," I say and even though I haven't thought twice about that before, for some reason, it felt weird to say it out loud.

I know where Noah works, but I have never been inside the building. I have dropped him off outside plenty of times when we had car issues over the years. But there has never been a reason for me to go inside of the building and inside his office though.

I do not like where Chloe is going with these questions, these accusations. She does not know my husband and she doesn't need to know about him either.

"Well, there's never been an opportunity for me to be at his job." I defend Noah, sitting up straighter. "Noah doesn't attend work parties or any other events outside of the office. He doesn't take lunch breaks there either. He comes home instead. I've dropped him off at his job plenty of times over the years."

"What did you say he does for work again?" Chloe raises her eyebrows.

"He's a marketing campaign director."

"And he has to travel a lot for that?"

"Sometimes."

"Interesting," Chloe mutters.

In ten years, I have never doubted Noah's faithfulness and I am not about to doubt him now because of one pessimistic woman who clearly has an issue with men.

"He's not one of those guys," I tell her defensively.

"Hey, I'm not trying to be a negative friend." She gives me another empathetic smile and rests her hand on my knee.

"It's just…I've had bad experiences with men," Chloe says, removing her hand from my knee.

Yeah, that's obvious.

Chloe crosses her right leg over the left like the conversation is going to turn serious. "If Noah ends up being like one of those guys, I'll be here for you."

"Okay. Thanks." I smile, uncertain of what she just meant. "Well, thanks for dinner. I'll see you tomorrow or something."

I leave her backyard and walk around to the front, then across the road to my house.

Chloe did not have a boyfriend when she first moved into the house across from me.

I have never seen the same guy go into Chloe's house more than one time.

And I am positive about that.

Over the few months of her living here, I have counted four different men who have walked into her house and never walk out. Not the same person.

If a guy had ever lived with Chloe in the house across from mine, I would have noticed. Especially when she first moved in. Besides the moving company she hired, Chloe moved in alone. No friends. No family.

Chloe lied to me tonight. And now I need to know why.

6

J u l y   1 9 ^{t h}   S u n d a y

I've had bad experiences with men.

What bad experiences was Chloe talking about?

"Why lie about living with a guy when it never happened?" I ask Noah, who is sitting across from me at our kitchen table.

I sip my coffee, my right leg shakes. I feel jittery. I want to know more about Chloe. She's hiding something.

"How do you know that she's lying about that?" Noah asks while scarfing down the last of his eggs.

He's not late for work. I don't know why he is eating so quickly.

Maybe it's because I am annoying him with what he probably thinks is a delusional theory.

"Because I would have noticed if a guy was living with her, even if it was for a short amount of time. Babe, you know that I like to look out the window when I'm working. I notice things in this neighborhood." I crease my forehead. "Something is up with Chloe. You know I have good instincts. I thought she was a stripper at first and I was kind of almost right about that. It turns out she works at a go-go bar downtown."

"So, she *is* a dancer?" Noah looks at me.

Sure. Now he sounds more interested in our conversation.

"No," I exhale. "She's a cocktail waitress. I mean, working at a bar with half-naked dancers is close enough to what I was originally thinking."

"How do you know she isn't lying about that too? Maybe she's actually a go-go dancer and didn't want to tell you the truth. Maybe she told you she served tables instead." He shrugs, focusing back on his food.

My eyes widen.

Shit. Noah could be right.

Chloe might have lied and said she was a waitress at a bar instead of admitting that she was a dancer because she was…embarrassed?

"That wouldn't make any sense," I think out loud, answering my own internal question.

Noah chuckles. I see him smiling at me from across the table.

"Can you not laugh at me? I'm serious." I cross my arms at my torso, leaning back in my chair.

"I'm not laughing at you. I just like when you get curious. You look cute when you're thinking."

"You have to admit I'm right about most

things." I smirk at his compliment, but then I realize I shouldn't sound so confident. "Except for that one time."

"I know." He smiles. "So, what do you think is going on with Chloe? Why do you think she's lying to you?"

"Well…" I hesitate.

He gives me that *where has your mind explored to now?* look.

"Don't laugh," I exhale.

"I would never laugh at you." Noah smiles.

I put my fork down on my plate, already regretting my decision to tell Noah my true thoughts, but here I go. "Chloe might be a serial killer."

A quick grin appears on Noah's face. "So, you're telling me that you think our neighbor is killing people and you still chose to hang out with her? Alone?"

"Of course that would be your response," I groan. "Let me explain!"

"I'm listening." Noah sits back in his chair, giving me his full attention.

Although his expression has already implied that he has made up his decision: *Whatever Ellie says is going to sound crazy.*

My husband never intends to diminish my words and opinions, but he can't hide his facial expressions or his tone of voice if he is disbelieving. No matter what the situation is, if he is skeptical, worried or even slightly doubtful of anything, it shows on his face.

"I've seen four different men go into Chloe's house on separate nights, okay?"

Noah nods. "Okay."

"The first time I noticed anything was about four months ago. I happen to see Chloe come home with a guy late at night when you were out of town for one of your campaigns."

"A one-night stand. Got it." Noah nods again.

"Yeah, sure." I refrain from rolling my eyes. "I was outside drinking my wine on the front porch when I saw them get out of her Jeep. I never saw the guy leave her house the next morning, but Chloe left without him."

Noah stares, clearly waiting for me to elaborate on my explanation.

"Then it happened three more times," I continue. "A few weeks later, Chloe came home with another man, but I never saw him leave her house the next morning either."

"Ellie…" Noah's grin is appearing again. It's not a condescending grin, but a *'let's not do this'* supportive type of grin. And it gives me the urge to slap it off his face right now.

"The same thing happened last month with a different guy. He walked through her front door one night and never left the next day. Then I saw her with another man only two weeks ago. It was the night before you told me to introduce myself to her. Remember, I said there was someone in her house that morning? I never saw the man leave after you went to work that morning and I was home all day."

Noah is staring at me, but he isn't saying anything.

"Babe, nobody ever leaves that woman's house. Ever." I nearly whine out of irritation.

His blank stare is highly frustrating.

"Did you ask Chloe about any of these men

that you saw?"

Finally, he speaks.

"Well, no. It's not like I told the woman that I was watching her." I huff.

"You were probably just not home or paying attention when those guys left. Or you weren't awake. I bet they called a ride in the middle of the night, and you never noticed. It's not like you're watching her house *all* the time."

"Well…" I hesitate. "I *have* checked our camera footage once or twice."

"Babe!" Noah groans, disappointed that I intruded on our neighbor's privacy.

"I was curious." I grin. "I played back the footage a few times. The camera has never caught any of Chloe's *guests* leave."

"Our camera isn't installed to watch our neighbors. It's in case anyone breaks into our home." Noah shakes his head.

"I know this," I singsong, smirking. "But you know that our camera always records when a car drives by or when anyone walks on our street. There is no way it would have missed each time someone walked out of Chloe's house other than Chloe. And there is no other way out of her house. Even if you leave through the backyard, you still have to walk around to the front yard to leave the neighborhood. So how did those men leave?" I cross my arms at my torso.

"I don't know what to tell you, babe." Noah gets up from the table, then walks over to kiss me before he heads out of the front door. "I'll only be at the office for a couple of hours today."

"I wish you didn't have to go in on the

weekend," I sigh.

"I know." He kisses my forehead. "Just a couple more months and then I'm requesting vacation once I'm done traveling."

I never cared about Noah working overtime on the weekends when it comes to preparation for his marketing trips, as he is doing today but ever since Chloe's comment, my feelings have slightly changed.

Only slightly though. I still trust my husband. Nobody will ever change that.

After locking the front door once Noah leaves, I head to the kitchen. Time to pour a glass of wine and wait for Chloe to go to work.

As I am opening the blinds of my window, I am just in time to see Chloe walk out of her front door.

Wearing black jeans and a blue sweatshirt, she passes her Jeep and continues walking down the driveway. I am guessing she is checking her mail before she leaves for work.

I guess I can check my mail too.

I leave my house and walk down my driveway to my mailbox.

"Hey!" I wave at Chloe who is walking away from hers already.

"Oh, hey!" She turns around and walks back down her driveway, then across the street toward me. "I was going to knock on your door later, but since you're out here, I'll just ask you now. A couple of my friends from the bar are going out tomorrow night to get drinks since we're all off work. You said you wanted to get out of the house. You should come with us!"

When I offered to hang out with Chloe outside of her house, I did not want other people to be with us.

But, if this is a way to get close to her, then so be it.

"The Ghost bar? The place you work at?" I raise my eyebrows.

Chloe doesn't normally work at the bar Monday nights.

"Oh, no!" Chloe laughs. "I only go there when I'm getting paid. We're going to another bar, downtown on the strip. I don't know the name of the place. One of my coworkers invited me."

"Sounds good." I try to smile and sound excited.

"We're meeting at the bar around eleven tomorrow night. Just walk over to my place when you're done getting ready. I'll call us an Uber so we can both drink."

"Can't wait!" I nod with my fake enthusiasm, then we part ways.

I kind of regret walking outside just now because I have no desire to hang out with anybody besides Chloe tomorrow.

Not that I ever have a desire to socialize with anybody anyways.

Hell, tomorrow night is going to be challenging for me, but I am up for it.

Especially if that means I might catch a killer; a killer who is becoming my new friend.

7

J u l y   2 0^{t h}   M o n d a y

I normally work only three days during the week, but I decided to pick up a shift this morning to get my mind off what's to come tonight.

However instead of calling customers, I open a tab next to my work portal online to search for local missing persons in Avery, Florida.

Even more shocking; this time, fourteen results show up.

There were thirteen people listed when I checked this page only about two weeks ago…

Above Bianca, the teenager who is still missing, I see a new face appear on the list.

Steven Shang. 28-year-old male. 6'1. Reported missing on July 7th. Last seen by his brother in the downtown area of Avery.

But I checked this database about two weeks ago and Steven was not on this list.

I also saw a guy step out of Chloe's Jeep, go inside her house, and never come out about two weeks ago; the same morning when I first introduced myself to her.

That was a Sunday on July 5th.

Steven Shang disappeared two days later: July 7th.

It was too dark outside for me to see the face of the man who got out of Chloe's Jeep that night, but I slightly remember what he looked like. He looked in shape. He wore a dark T-shirt and dark jeans, and he was noticeably a lot taller than Chloe is. I would say he was around at least five foot nine. Maybe six feet tall.

And Chloe is five foot six according to her license, and that must be correct because I am five foot five. She's not that much taller than me.

The height next to Steven Shang's photo says he is six foot one. I expand the image of Steven to get a better look at him.

Have I seen him before?

Or do I just want to think I saw him before?

I open a new tab online to search for his Facebook profile by looking up his first and last name and selecting the location: Avery, Florida in the search option.

After scrolling past a couple of results, I find the *Steven Shang* that I am looking for.

As he stands in his profile photo, I see that he's in shape; not overly muscular, yet definitely toned. Brown eyes. Dark brunette hair in the style of a buzzcut. His last post was from almost over a month ago: a picture of him fishing off a pier with two other guys.

There are a few other posts and comments from his friends which say they wonder where he is and how much they miss him. Except nobody has commented any speculations as to what could have happened to him. Everyone seems confused about his disappearance.

Under Steven's friends list, I type the name *Chloe Jones.*

They aren't friends.

Wait... I should have done this sooner. I need to look for Chloe's social media presence.

I have my own social media profiles, but when it comes to interaction, I do the bare minimum. That's why I never thought about following or friending Chloe on any profiles until now.

Ten results come up under the search results for *Chloe Jones in Avery, FL* on Facebook.

I scroll through the profile photos until I find the Chloe that I know. Or think I know, I should say.

Although her picture doesn't look so recent, I can tell this profile is hers. She has a bit more weight on her face in her photo and her hair is colored charcoal black instead of the dark brunette like it is now.

And her profile is set to private.

All I can see is her first name, age, and her profile photo which was posted last year according to the timestamp when I expand the image. The comments are set to private.

I think twice about friending her so soon. I should wait until after we hang out at the bar, so it won't be awkward. Chloe should not know that I was searching for her online already. That is technically stalking, and I am not a stalker like Noah jokingly indicated.

Call me an observer instead.

And now it is time for me to observe Chloe's Instagram.

But on Instagram, no profile under her name matches the Chloe I want to find. I guess she uses a different username other than her real name. I will have to get that out of her when we're drinking at the bar tonight.

I click back to Steven's profile to look at his photo again. *Seriously, he is starting to look familiar the more I look at him.*

Maybe I've seen him in the grocery store or something…

Or maybe I am starting to overthink again, like my therapist told me I did after Laura died.

It's been about two years since I had a session. I wonder what my therapist would say if I told her about my new theory.

Would she tell me that I am imagining a situation because I am bored and trying to make it come to life for some excitement?

That's basically what she said before. Amongst a few other things, these few words are what stuck with me; "*You unintentionally let your anxiety become an unhealthy obsession. You began imagining things to happen when they weren't there because that's all you could focus on. You started fearing the worst in everything around you after Laura passed away.*"

I agreed with my therapist at the time because it was true. *I fucked up.* I did let my imagination get the best of me even though it was not intentional.

I think if I talked to my therapist now, she would say the same thing is happening to me again; I am letting my anxiety become an unhealthy obsession. I am imagining things.

But this time I would not agree. Because now I have a bit of evidence. It's not much but it *is* something.

It is something more than when I made a ridiculous assumption that led me to see a therapist in the first place.

And this time, I will make sure to keep my thoughts to myself.

At least I will for now.

8

For the first time in about ten years, I spent four excruciating hours awkwardly standing in a sardine packed bar with Chloe and two annoying women that I think were in their early twenties. Chloe introduced me to them, but I don't remember either of their names. Nor do I care to remember them either.

The bar was so crowded, I started sweating even though I was not wearing much clothing. A black crop top suffocated my breasts, and a short red pin skirt hugged my hips. Noah loved what I was wearing before I walked over to Chloe's.

He also reminded me that Chloe is my new friend, and that I should stop thinking she is a killer.

"If you really think that woman is dangerous, then please don't hang out with her," Noah softly asked me when I was getting ready for the night. "I want you to have friends but just be careful."

I proceeded to assure him that my thoughts of Chloe killing anyone were no longer in my mind.

Yes, I know I lied to my husband. And no, I do not like it and am not proud of it either.

But I had to lie. If Noah knows that I am still suspicious of Chloe, he will suggest that I call my therapist again.

And I don't want that to happen.

Even though I feel terrible about lying, it was nice to see my husband get excited to see me dressed up.

Marriage is simple, but also a bit complicated. When one person hurts in the relationship, the other does. I was not going to tear my husband's excitement down by telling him the truth. Then I would feel bad for upsetting him.

I do admit Chloe is fun to be around. However, her friends whose names I do not care to remember, were not as enjoyable company. On another note, one thing I observed about Chloe: She didn't seem to act any different around her friends than she acts around me. She had plenty of drinks except she was not as drunk as them and thankfully, not nearly as chatty either.

Apparently, the women also work at the Ghost Bar with Chloe, and they are waitresses too. I was happy when the taller woman out of Chloe's friends decided to leave because she had some appointment early the next morning. She said what it was but I don't remember or care.

Twenty minutes later, the other young twenty called herself a ride while Chloe and I jumped in our

Uber to get back home. I guess her friend lived the opposite way of us which was better for me.

I was glad to be alone with Chloe again.

Once we were on our way home, I casually asked Chloe for her social media, and she gave me her Instagram. We started following each other right away.

By the time we left the bar, I was tipsy but still lucid enough to keep my guard up. Our ride dropped us off outside of our houses about twenty minutes ago.

I have not changed out of these tight clothes yet because Noah is already asleep in our bedroom, and I don't want to wake him. So I decided to lay down on the couch and do some investigating.

The lights are off in my living room and the blinds on the window are open only slightly enough to see Chloe's driveway. I do not expect to see anything shady over there because she is probably passed out sleeping already, but you never know.

Now that we are following each other on Instagram, it's time to observe Chloe's profile.

She has two hundred and two followers, and she follows only half of them back. Her last post was from three weeks ago; A *life is short, go drink margarita* quote that is typed over a picture of a palm tree.

Two weeks before that, she posted a selfie while making a pasta dish in her kitchen captioned: *Loving my life in my new home.*

The rest of her content varies from random photos and videos of food, drinks, occasional photos of herself (none in her Jack's T-shirt or Ghost Bar cocktail uniform) and images of sunrises from the driver side of her Jeep.

The latest sunrise post from two and a half weeks ago is captioned: *The only perk of getting off work at five o'clock in the morning are the beautiful sunrises on the way home.*

For a potential serial killer, Chloe sounds kind of optimistic.

Wait a second. Where are the two women who I met tonight? I don't see any photos of them with Chloe on her profile.

Actually, Chloe is not pictured with anybody.

No other friends. No family. No ex-boyfriends… I only see selfies, sunsets, food, and random quotes on her profile. Nobody has tagged her in any photos or videos either.

Maybe her setting for tagged content is set to private.

I move my search from my cell phone to the computer on my desk. Time to look at Avery's missing reported persons list again.

Fourteen results still show.

When I was explaining to Noah why I was suspicious of Chloe at first, I realized that I might have listed off a pattern.

I saw four different men go into Chloe's house on separate nights. I can't recall the exact dates, but I know I saw her invite each man over a few weeks apart from each other.

And I didn't start to notice her guests until about three or four months ago… shortly after she moved in.

All these men went missing in between almost a three week to one month timespan from each other. And they are all over the height of five foot nine…

That also looks like a pattern.

Theo Dian. Age 29. 6'0.
Reported on April 19th by his mother after not hearing from him for a day.

Ryan Davis. Age 25. 5'9.
Reported missing on May 12th by his sister.

Devon Gomes. Age 31. 5'9.
Reported missing on June 17th. Last seen getting drinks at a bar downtown with a friend.

Steven Shang. Age 28. 6'1.
Reported missing on July 7th. Last seen by his brother in the downtown area of Avery.

The reports for Steven and Devon state they were last seen in Downtown Avery before they both went missing.

I view the calendar to compare the days.

April 19th – Friday
May 12th – Tuesday
June 17th – Wednesday
July 7th – Tuesday

Devon disappeared on a Wednesday while Ryan and Steven went missing on a Tuesday.

Devon and Steven were both last seen downtown...

Chloe works Tuesdays and Wednesdays at the Ghost Go-Go bar. And the Ghost Go-Go bar is located on the strip with all the other bars and clubs…downtown.

"No fucking way." I sit back in my chair staring in awe of my computer screen.

I know my mind can wander. I know that I can imagine situations that do not exist. I know I made a mistake in the past because of that…

But this…this is right in my face.

I am staring at a pattern in these men's disappearances.

But is it a pattern of a serial killer?

What else would it be?

I don't hope that any of these men are dead… but what if they are?

Could Chloe really be capable of killing? What would be her motive?

"I've had bad experiences with men. "

What was she trying to tell me?

And what is the true definition of a serial killer anyways?

I skim through Google to find my answer.

From the results, I summarize; ***A serial killer is a person who murders three or more persons with no apparent motive, typically following a predictable pattern.***

"Hey, babe."

"Holy shit!" Noah's voice startles me. I leap up from my computer and turn off the screen.

"I didn't hear you come home. What are you doing on your computer this late? Are you okay?"

"Oh, I couldn't fall asleep yet. I didn't want to wake you up." I turn off my computer, then walk over to kiss him.

"Did you have fun with your friends tonight?"

He reaches his arms around my waist.

"I did," I smile and kiss him.

As much as I want to continue my search, I follow Noah into the bedroom. *Hopefully, he didn't see what was on my computer screen.*

9

Why would Chloe lie to me about an ex-boyfriend living in her house when she has only ever lived there alone? She lied to me in such a casual way, if I didn't already know that she was lying, I might have believed her.

That's why from now on, I am going to make sure that I catch her in whatever lie she decides to tell me next.

So, how do I do that without giving off that I am suspicious of her?

The answer comes easy from the internet.

There are experts in the psyche and while I do not obtain a psychology degree or any type of degree at all, thanks to the internet; I can become knowledgeable on better understanding the mind too.

At least, I can try.

The first key to understanding liars: you *can't spot lies*, but you *can spot a liar*.

And you can spot a bad or a good liar through multiple ways.

1. *Their eye movement.*

A liar will look away when they are speaking during an important part of their lie. Their eyes move away from the person they are talking to at the specific point of when they are lying. Then they regain eye contact at the part of when they aren't lying. Here is an example:

Question: *"Did you go to the festival last night?"*

Answer: *"No. I wasn't at the festival. I was at home."*

If the person kept eye contact when they responded: *"No. I wasn't at the festival"*, they weren't lying about not being at the festival because in truth, they weren't there.

But if they looked away when they said, *"was at home"*, they were lying about being at home. In truth, they were actually somewhere else and not at home.

2. *Body Language*

Is the person's body stiff or are they shifting when answering a question? If the person is fidgeting, focus on when they are moving their body. Are they shifting their weight during the moment they are being asked the question they intend to lie about? Or are they shifting during their answer? Are they doing something specific when speaking? Like touching their hair, crossing their feet, or twitching their lips?

Chloe crossed her legs when she offered to be there for me if Noah ends up turning into an asshole. Even after I insisted that he is not like that.

3.   *Hand and body gestures.*

This goes along with body language as well. Liars exaggerate their gestures when talking by using their hands and body.

4.   *Time.*

How long does it take for the person to answer your question? If the suspected liar is not prepared for the question and how they are going to respond with a lie, or if they are a bad liar, they may take a moment to answer. They are giving themselves time to think about their next lie. They are thinking about their follow up to the first lie to continue their made-up story, so that their lie can keep going.

When you start one lie, it becomes hard to stop. One lie normally leads into another. And another. And another.

5. A good liar doesn't tell too much but they tell just enough at the appropriate time.

They divert the conversation away from the topic they do not want to speak about.

Chloe briefly mentioned an ex-boyfriend that I know she lied to me about. She never went on to tell me more about him.

6. Their face.

Is the person sweating? Is their face pale? Are they holding a smile too long or not long enough?

Now that I have all this information, I need to take my time and observe Chloe. I can't jump to conclusions just yet. I need to remain patient, which is something I have never been successful in.

Noah likes to remind me so all the time.

I minimize my bookmark labeled *LIAR INFO* on my computer and click over to my work portal. I logged in half an hour ago after Noah left for work.

Thankfully he never uses my computer. Because if he saw that I have an online bookmark with a list of websites about liars, he'd call my therapist for me, instead of only suggesting it.

"I can do this." I give myself a peptalk out loud before putting my headset on to connect to my first customer call of the day.

"Hello?" The sound of the ocean waves fills the background noise behind the customer on the other end of the phone.

"Hello. My name is Ellie. I'm calling from Rodally's Collections Services. May I please speak to Nicholas Wilson?"

"Yes. Sorry, it's a bit loud here," he yells over the waves.

"That's okay, sir. I'm calling because you have a delinquent payment due in the amount of one hundred and fifty dollars that is a week late. I am calling to see how you would like to make the payment today."

"I am currently out at sea. The waters are getting rough, hold on one moment! Mayday! Mayday! Hold on ma'am. I need to get my ship from sink-

"FUCK YOU!" I shout into my headset even though I know I just yelled at a robot.

Angered, I throw my headpiece across the living room.

Fucking Robo calls. People pay for these services when collection agents or any spam calls come in. They're pre-recorded ridiculous responses to aggravate us callers.

When I first began working as an agent, these types of calls were entertaining to me. That lasted all of about three months. Now the robo calls just annoy me.

Through my window, I see that Chloe hasn't left for work at the market yet, so I send her a text.

You home?

A minute later, she replies.

Yep. I'm here.

I walk over to Chloe's house, accepting her reply as an invitation to knock on her front door.

A few minutes later, we are sitting in her backyard with fresh brewed coffee that she made for us.

"I am so fed up with my job. I clocked out after the first call." Sipping my drink, I peer out into the woods behind her backyard.

What a convenient place to dispose of a body.

"Won't that get you fired?" Chloe asks.

"I really don't care." I shrug. "So, not to be nosy but I was wondering…" I hesitate. I did not think this one through but here it goes. I need to bring up Steven without directly bringing him up. "You still dating that guy you brought home a little while ago?"

Chloe stiffens. Her guard is up. She's quiet.

Chloe sets her drink on the patio deck beside her chair. Her eye contact is toward her feet. Not on me.

Three seconds of silence go by before she speaks. "I didn't know you're a night owl."

Turning the question around on me. *Liar.*

"I don't sleep these days," I respond.

She looks at me, shrugging. "I guess he was fun. We're not dating though. It was just a one-time thing. That was about two weeks ago though. Why are you bringing him up all of a sudden?" She chuckles nervously. "I told you that I'm not dating anyone serious right now."

"Oh, small talk, I guess. I don't know. I had a glass of wine before I came over." I fake a laugh, wishing I weren't as sober as I truly am. "Guess I forgot what you said before. Sorry."

"You drink wine first thing in the morning?" She raises her eyebrows.

"How do you think I normally get through those robo calls?"

Chloe laughs, relaxing her body.

Wait… it's a quarter to ten o'clock already. Why isn't she at work yet?

I look at her black pants and blue tank top. "So, what are you up to today? You scheduled at the market?" I ask, as if I don't already know that she is supposed to be there by now.

"Yeah. I'm going to leave as soon as we're done with our coffee. I woke up right before you texted me. My alarm didn't go off on time. I'm not in such a rush to get there anyway."

Chloe kept eye contact with me the whole time. She didn't hesitate. She didn't cross her leg. She had a quick answer. From my recent research, I think she is telling the truth.

"So, what are your plans for the rest of the day now that you have a day off?" Chloe asks.

"I'm going to the gym, then I might do some shopping."

I can learn to be a liar too. Neither of those things are on my agenda for the day.

My day will consist of furthering my investigation into Chloe.

And by doing that, I first need to speak with the person who reported Steven Shang missing.

10

July 22nd

Wednesday

My mind can imagine extreme situations that do not exist.

Bad things consume my thoughts. I think of horrifying events even though I don't want those events to come true.

These thoughts began right after Laura died. She died in a car accident due to a freshly paved and wet road in a storm. Since her unexpected death was out of my control, it left me with a tremendous amount of anxiety. I began to worry about everything else in my life that is also out of my control.

This explanation came from my therapist.

I worried before Laura was alive, but I admit my anxiety immensely developed right after her death. But even though I am aware of how my mind can react, I know that my instincts are strong.

And even when I don't want to be right, often times I am.

Except for what happened two years ago.

But besides then, my instincts are telling me that I should be cautious of Chloe. My instincts are also telling me there is a killer who is targeting men in Avery, and it is not a coincidence that two of those men went missing in the same area.

That is why I am heading to talk to Steven Shang's brother, Henry; the person who reported him missing.

I easily found Henry through Steven's friends on Facebook.

Instead of messaging Henry, I went a step further and searched for his phone number and address online. His number was not listed publicly. However, his recent address was.

At least, I hope this is his recent address.

I just parked my truck in front of a small two-story yellow apartment building a few blocks away from my neighborhood. Henry is supposed to live on the second floor in apartment ten.

After I climb the staircase outside of the building, I walk down the hallway past a few blue doors until I spot the number *ten*.

A tall bald-headed man who is wearing a blue T-shirt and black basketball shorts appears behind the door only a moment after I knock.

Even without the hair, it is obvious that he is related to Steven. Henry just looks like a slightly older version of him, which he is.

According to Henry's profile, I found out that he is thirty-two years old.

He looks at me up and down. "Can I help you?"

"Hi. I'm sorry to bother you. My name is Ellie. I have a few questions about your brother's disappearance. I saw that you reported him missing."

Henry's forehead creases. "Who are you? How did you get my address?"

That's a reasonable question, so I tell him that I am an upcoming crime investigation blogger.

Thanks to my liar research, I have come prepared. I saw Steven pop up as a recent missing person in Avery.

"My first case is looking into local disappearances here in town, and I believe your brother's disappearance might fit into a pattern, but I have questions before I can confirm my theory," I say confidently.

After a moment of contemplation, Henry decides to believe me and invites me into his apartment. "My name's Henry. Nice to meet you."

Yes, I know what your name is.

Henry leads me into the living room. He gestures for me to sit on the roughed up black leather couch which faces a flat screen TV that is mounted on the wall. A brown recliner chair is arranged on the left side of the sofa. "Want a beer?" he asks as he heads toward the kitchen.

I decline the drink as I sit on his sofa.

After getting himself a beer, Henry sits in the brown chair. "So, what do you want to know?"

"Okay. First, can you tell me what happened in the few hours before you reported Steven missing?" I shift uncomfortably.

"We went out drinking and he left with some

girl. Never came home the next day." Henry sips his beer, seemingly annoyed by the situation, the simplicity in how quickly Steven left.

"Where were you guys out drinking at?" I ask.

"A bar downtown."

Henry's either an introvert or he is suspicious of me because he's only responding with short answers.

Or maybe he is drunk. I am just starting to notice a bunch of empty beer cans on the floor by the sofa.

"Do you remember the name of the place you were at?" I ask, gritting my teeth.

"That go-go bar. Ghost something."

"Ghost Go-Go bar?" I repeat with my head low.

He nods, putting his beer on the table. "Yeah, that place."

No fucking way.

"The woman that Steven was with that night, was her name Chloe?" I sit up straighter.

"Like I got her name," Henry scoffs a sarcastic laugh. "Hell, I don't even remember what her face looked like. I was pretty drunk. So was Steven."

"What night were you guys there?"

"Tuesday night. July 7th. I woke up the next morning and realized he never came home. I tried calling him, but the phone went to voicemail. That's when I went to the police station." Henry shakes his head and picks his phone up off the coffee table. "I could call it right now and it will still go to voicemail."

"So, the police didn't make you wait twenty-four hours to report Steven missing?" I ask because if they did, then the dates that are listed under the disappearances on the missing persons list might not be accurate.

"I thought the cops would tell me about some bullshit like that, but I still showed up to the station anyway. The police told me that isn't a law in Florida, the whole waiting twenty-four to forty-eight hours before having to report someone missing. Apparently, there isn't any certain waiting period to report a person missing."

"Interesting," I mumble. "Do you remember the woman you saw Steven with that night; if she worked at the bar?"

Henry shakes his head. "I don't think so. She kept bringing Steven drinks though." He looks down, thinking back to that night. "I'm not really sure. The whole night's a blur. Like I said, I was pretty hammered."

He may have been hammered but maybe a photo will jog his memory.

I pull out my phone from my purse to show him a screenshot of one of Chloe's selfies that I took off her profile earlier. "Do you recognize this woman?"

Henry leans in to look at my phone screen as I hold it out toward him, then shakes his head. "Don't think so."

"Are you sure?" I ask again.

"Yeah. I'm sure. But why? You think that woman is a suspect or something?" He gestures toward my phone with a nod.

I shouldn't tell him who Chloe is. His brother

could be fine and now I'm raising more concern. I do not want to be that person. I'm intervening in a situation that I probably shouldn't...

But then again, what if my theory is right though? What if what I'm doing will bring Steven back?

Or at least find out what happened to him?

"I really don't know anything yet. I have more investigating to do. I'm just kind of going off a hunch."

"You think that woman's just kidnapping men around here?" He eyes me up and down, disbelieving.

"That or killing them," I respond frankly.

I didn't intend to flat out imply his brother could be dead but if Henry wants to act so doubtful of what I am saying, then so be it.

"Well, shit..." He rests his elbows on his knees. "Wow. A female serial killer. I'm sure there's a shitload of them these days."

Given my theory lately he may be right, and I might just be living across from one.

11

Since I learned about Steven's whereabouts the night he went missing, it's time to investigate the disappearances of Theo, Devon, and Ryan.

Starting with Theo; after about ten minutes of scrolling through various social media profiles under the name *Theo Dian,* I found him. He lives in New York. He flew to Avery a month ago for his friend's wedding. The most recent posts on Theo's profile were tagged pictures posted from the groom of the wedding, Benton Peterson.

Using my fake crime blogger lie, I sent a message to Benton. I asked him to simply explain what happened in the hours before Theo went missing. Maybe he could tell me if he knew where he was at. I sent that message only an hour ago, but I have not got a reply yet.

Until I do receive a response, I continue my investigation next, with Devon.

On his missing person's report, it says he was last seen getting drinks with a friend in Downtown Avery.

Through some more social media searching, I found Devon's profile. Then I found his friend, Adam who tagged him in a post only a week ago.

The post reads:

I just thought Devon would be back by now. The police haven't done shit since I reported him missing. It's been over a month already since he disappeared. If anyone knows of anything, speak up!

The comments beneath Adam's post didn't offer any information that was of use to me so I showed up to his job.

He openly posts photos of himself in uniform and checks into the diner weekly, so it wasn't difficult to find him.

"Table for one," I say to the hostess after entering the diner. "Is it possible that I could sit in Adam's section?"

The hostess briefly looks at the seating chart on the stand before leading me through the busy dining room.

A couple of minutes later, Adam greets me as his waiter, and I immediately get right to my point and tell him the same lie that I told Henry.

My fake upcoming crime blog story works once again. Adam eagerly tells me he'll be right back after offering me a drink. I only ask for water.

Minutes later, he walks past me with a tray of food and a glass of water. He delivers the meals to a couple sitting two booths over, then comes back to my booth and places the water in front of me as he sits down in the booth. "I got to be quick but if you're really trying to help find Devon, then what do you want to know?"

I like his enthusiasm.

"I'm sorry to bother you while you're working. I'll try to make this quick," I say. "I saw your post about Devon on Facebook. You reported him missing to the police about a month ago, right?"

"Yes, I did," Adam says. "Devon's roommate said he didn't come home the night we were out drinking. When he didn't answer the phone the next day, I started worrying. I called his mom and she said she hadn't heard from him. I waited nearly until midnight the next day before I called the police."

"That was June 17th the night he went missing, right? Where were you out drinking?" I ask.

"Correct. We were at a club downtown. Club Fate."

Not the Go-Go bar, but damn well close enough to it. Club Fate is located only a block away from Ghost Go-Go.

I've never been to Club Fate, but I did go to the bar right next to it. Chloe took me there the night we got drinks with her friends.

"That was a Wednesday night, right?" I ask even though he just confirmed the date to me.

"Right."

"Did you leave the club with Devon that night?"

"Nah," Adam shakes his head. "We both found these two chicks, then we split off. He left about a half hour before I did. He told me he'd see me tomorrow," he sighs. "That never happened. I figured he was going back home with her. I thought he went to her place at first but then he didn't answer his phone the next day. I don't know what happened to him, man."

"Do you remember what the woman who Devon was with looked like?"

"Not too much. Her hair was short. It was black. She wore a lot of makeup." He shakes his head. "I don't really remember her in detail. I was paying attention to my girl. Not his." He wrinkles his nose. "Why are you asking about her?"

The only time I saw Chloe wear a lot of makeup was during the night I went drinking with her and those two annoying women. But Chloe wasn't wearing so much makeup that it looked excessive though. And Chloe is brunette. Her hair falls a little past her shoulders. Not short and black like Adam just described…

"Is this her?" I ask when showing the screenshot of Chloe off my phone to Adam.

Squinting, he leans over the table. Then he shakes his head as he looks at my phone. "Nah, not her."

"Are you sure?"

"It wasn't her." He sits back in the booth.

I put my phone back in my purse. "Did you tell the police about the woman Devon met that night? She was the last person that was seen with him, right? Did they question her?"

"Well, yeah," he shrugs. "I told the cops about her. But I didn't even get her name. How could they question her?" He sits up again. "Wait… do you think she has something to do with Devon going missing?"

Well…yes. In my opinion, it seems like common sense to question the last person who was seen with Devon before he went missing.

"Women can be suspects too," I mumble.

"Shit…" Adam sighs.

Really, people overlook the capabilities of women. Henry did and now so is Adam.

"The police never suggested that. The cop just asked me what we did that night. I told them what I told you." He huffs. "Shit. I wonder if I can find out who she is…"

"Maybe you *can*," I say.

"How?" Adam squints his eyes, confused.

"Try going back to Club Fate. Maybe that woman goes there often. See if you'll spot her there another night."

I am just simply suggesting what I would do if I were in his situation. I would go to Club Fate and look for the woman myself if I had a better description of her. I'm tempted to ask him if I can tag along but what would I tell Noah?

"Good idea" Adam stands up. "I guess it's worth a try. *Damn.* I wish I had thought of that earlier. I think I might head there tonight."

Good. I have his mind running. Maybe he'll be of use to me.

"Can we exchange numbers? If you see her again, can you let me know?"

Adam agrees and I leave him a five-dollar bill even though I only took a few sips of water. He thanks me after insisting that my money is unnecessary, but I leave it on the table for him anyways.

THE WOMAN I BEFRIENDED

My next destination is Ryan Davis' sister's house.

12

Just like I found Steven, Devon, and Theo's social media profiles; Ryan was easy to find too. And his profile led me to his older sister, Sherry Lance. She's three years older than him and lives in the next town over which is about half an hour drive from Avery.

Through an online search using her first and last name which is different from Ryan because Sherry is married, I found Sherry's current address.

After parking my truck in a cobblestone driveway, I step out in front of a one-story white house with several large windows that decorate the exterior. A swing set is in the front of the yard. A blue bicycle with training wheels lies on its side by the garage. Sherry must have kids.

I kind of hope they are at school because I don't need her to be distracted when I ask my questions.

Once I approach the red front door of the home and knock, the door opens to reveal a red and swollen face behind it a moment later.

"Uh, hi," I choke on my words, not ready to deal with the hysteria so soon. "I'm here about Ryan. Are you the one who reported him missing? Are you Sherry, his sister?"

"Yes! Do you know where he is?" She looks at me with wide eyes full of hope that I am about to shatter.

"N--no," I stutter. "I am so sorry to bother you, but I have a few questions about your brother's disappearance. It will only take a few minutes of your time."

She wipes her tears before crossing her arms. Her demeanor has turned defensive now. "Who are you? Why are you asking about Ryan?"

"I should have started with that. Sorry." I exhale. "My name is Ellie. I am starting an investigation blog on local disappearances, and I believe your brother could fit into a pattern—"

"A pattern? What do you mean by a pattern? Are you saying my brother could be… dead?" She lowers her head, staring at me.

"N--no!" I wave my hand, shaking my head. *Well, yes…but I won't tell her that.* "I just have a few questions."

She looks me up and down, giving me the sense that she is going to call the police or tell me to fuck off until she decides to open the door and invite me in.

"My names Sherry." She reaches her hand out toward me. I return the handshake.

She leads me through a short hallway inside of her house where she introduces her husband, Kane. He is eyeing Sherry with obvious and understandable confusion.

He is probably thinking; *Who the hell is this woman? Why is a stranger in his house?*

"She might help find Ryan," Sherry answers her husband's thoughts, and he nods in agreement.

Another benefit of marriage; you learn telepathy.

Kane follows us to the kitchen table. He sits down next to Sherry, immediately resting his palm on her hand on top of the table. I smile at the gesture. I am also smiling because their kids aren't around either.

Good. No distractions.

"Alright. So like I said, I won't take up that much of your time," I begin. "Can I ask you, what do you think happened to Ryan the night he disappeared?"

Sherry sighs. "Well, that's the thing. I'm not entirely sure. Ryan is not the type to get into a fight or cause trouble. Ryan is-- I don't know…" She struggles to find her words. "I can only imagine what happened. The three of us," She nods toward her husband. "We were out having drinks together because I got a promotion at my job. So, we were celebrating with him. Ryan has always been so supportive of me." She sniffles.

"Anyways, Ryan met a woman and danced with her all night which wasn't unusual. If he meets a woman or if he sees his buddies when we're out, he usually ditches us for them. I'm thinking he got lost on his way back home, stumbling, still drunk. Maybe someone hit him and drove away?" She inhales sharply. "Nobody wanted to hurt him. He's such a great guy… annoying, but he -- he's my brother, you know? I just… I want him to come home. I know he didn't leave town on his own will. And especially not without telling me first. Something happened to him."

"Do you think Ryan left the bar with the woman you saw him with that night? Did you see them leave together?" I ask, summarizing.

"We didn't see them leave together. But he was with her right before Kane and I left." She looks at her husband who concurs by nodding. "I went to Ryan's place the next morning and asked his neighbors if they saw him come home the night before, but nobody noticed anything. I even went inside his apartment. It didn't look like he came home that night."

"And so that's when you called the cops?" I ask.

"Yeah." Sherry nods, sniffling.

"What did the police do besides list him on the missing persons database? Did they go check out his apartment or ask the neighbors if they had seen your brother come home?"

Sherry shakes her head; no. Tears are starting to flow.

I need to wrap this up already. I feel terrible for causing this woman to cry but at the same time, I needed my answers.

"So, you both saw the woman Ryan was dancing with though? What did she look like?"

"She had long blonde hair. Tan skin. I think she was about my height," Sherry answers.

"How tall are you?"

Sherry is definitely taller than me which means she is also taller than Chloe.

"5'8," Sherry answers.

Despite the height difference, I grab my phone out of my purse to show Sherry and Kane the screenshot of Chloe. "Does this woman look familiar from that night?"

Sherry leans over the table, then shakes her head. "Not at all."

Kane shakes his head. "Don't know who that is."

"And where were you guys celebrating your promotion at? What was the place called?" I ask as I put my phone on the table.

"We were at a bar," Sherry says. "It's sort of like a club. The Ghost bar downtown with the go-go dancers. You've heard of it?"

"It's called Ghost Go-Go," Kane chimes in.

But I already knew the name.

And I think my face just turned pale and Sherry is noticing. Kane is starting to notice too.

"Why?" She straightens up, concerned.

"And it was on a Tuesday night you were all there, right? May 12th?" I ask, not intentionally trying to rudely ignore her question.

Silently exchanging looks, both Sherry and Kane nod.

"And you're both positive you didn't see the woman in the picture I showed you?" I ask them both one more time.

Again, they both nod slowly.

Kane is starting to look more skeptical of me than he did when I first walked in, so I ask to give Sherry my number in case she hears anything new.

Thankfully they don't press me for more information because I honestly wouldn't know what else to say and we exchange numbers.

Now it's time I head home and put all of my evidence against Chloe together. Hopefully Theo's friend will message me back soon and then I'll have enough information to make my next move.

AUGUST

13

According to the pattern that I identified in Theo, Ryan, Devon and Steven's disappearances, somebody, presumably a male between his mid-twenties to early thirties should have gone missing by now.

Or they will go missing within the next few days.

But Chloe has not had any guests at her house recently besides last night when I slept over.

I told Noah that Chloe invited me for a girl's night. And I told Chloe that Noah left for a work trip yesterday morning. I told her it's hard to sleep without him, hoping she would invite me to sleep over, and she did.

I'm a bored lonely housewife, remember?

Again, I did not entirely lie to my husband. Chloe did invite me over. I just didn't tell him what I said to get the invite.

And I didn't lie to Chloe either. Noah left yesterday morning for the first of his three remaining trips this year which are never more than a few days long; like this first one. I have to pick him up from the airport tomorrow night.

If Chloe is a killer, then yes, I am well aware that I am out of my damn mind for sleeping inside of her house. Just me and her alone.

Except I didn't sleep at all last night. I laid awake on her couch until I was sure she was asleep in her bedroom, or at least until I thought she was sleeping. An hour after I saw the bedroom light turn off from under her door, I took a chance to snoop around.

Besides her bedroom, I searched everywhere in this house which consists of a one bedroom, one bath and a small closet laundry room. It only holds her washer and dryer.

I did not find any form of a weapon or blood stains in the place. No secret spaces. No odd objects. No attic or garage either. Nothing the true crime documentaries or any thriller movie has prepared me to look for.

But Chloe's backyard is not fenced in, and it leads right out to the woods.

The tree line begins only a few feet past her yard after a patch of dirt and grass. Chloe can walk right into the woods whenever she pleases. She has direct access to it.

If I were a killer and my backyard led out to a couple acres of woods, I would think that would be the best and most convenient spot to bury a body.

But how would I drag a dead body from this backyard into those woods though?

I wouldn't.

That would be impossible. There is no way I have enough strength to drag a six-foot-tall male from here to those woods. Which means it would be just as impossible for Chloe who is only an inch taller and only a couple pounds more than me.

However, if I lived on this property and owned a Jeep like Chloe does, I would utilize my vehicle and drive my victims right out into the woods. So, if I had a Jeep and lived here at Chloe's, how would I transport my victims to my Jeep without the neighbor's seeing?

I would have to drive around to the backyard and drag my victims through the sliding door.

Then I would put them in my Jeep.

Getting my victims in my Jeep would be difficult. But not nearly as difficult as it would be to carry or drag a dead body out through the woods on foot.

Then I would drive out of our neighborhood to one of the roads that parallel the woods, and I would pick a dirt trail that lead into them.

Both houses to the left and right of Chloe's have fenced in backyards and both families work all day. So, I guess they don't really see what she does here in Chloe's backyard.

But I'm home all day and I see what she does. And I've never seen her drive back here.

Sitting on the back porch of Chloe's patio now, I sip my coffee. She looks like she had a peaceful night's sleep.

Glad one of us did.

"Did your ex-boyfriend cheat on you?" I abruptly ask once she is sitting in the chair next to me.

Her body stiffens. One. Two. Three. Four seconds later, she responds. "How'd you know?"

Answering my question with another question: *Liar trait.*

"It was the first thing you suggested about Noah when I first met you," I shrug. "You told me you had bad experiences with men. I'm only assuming." I make an awkward empathetic expression. "Am I a jackass for assuming?"

I waited to bring this topic up until the morning instead of asking her about him last night. I made sure to make Chloe feel comfortable in my presence before making her uncomfortable.

She looks away from me and toward the woods, crossing her right leg over her left.

Liars do something specific when lying, like touching their hair or crossing their legs.

She crossed her legs when she told me she had bad experiences with men, like she's doing right now.

"No, it's okay," Chloe shrugs. "One of my ex's not only cheated on me once but three times. The guy after him beat the shit out of me and the guy after that became a lazy drunk that couldn't pay the bills."

Chloe held eye contact with me the entire time she was speaking. No fidgeting. No exaggerated movements. But her body is stiff, and she looks very uncomfortable.

I can't tell if she is lying.

By her explanation, it sounds like the lazy drunk was her most recent ex-boyfriend. The guy that supposedly lived in this house with her when she first moved in; The man who I do not think exists.

"The lazy drunk couldn't afford the rent here, huh?" I ease my way in.

Chloe shakes her head, letting out a hysterical laugh.

Liars exaggerate body gestures.

"I should have never let him move in with me. Good thing I never put him on the lease."

"Well…" I exhale. "You weren't lying when you said you had bad experiences with men."

She laughs, relaxing her body back against the chair. "I like you. You're very blunt."

"My best friend used to say that." I smile, almost forgetting Laura would tell me the same thing until I just heard it again. She was the nicer, optimistic half of me.

"She sounds cool. Does she live around here?" Chloe asks.

"She's dead." My response prompts Chloe smile to drop.

"Shit. I'm sorry to hear that." She gives me that annoying look of pity I always get when I mention my best friend died to anyone. That's normally why grievers don't mention a person's death right away. We get that look that Chloe is giving me, and we don't know what to do with it. It's awkward.

If you tell a person someone died, they will most likely say, *I'm sorry.*

And then what am I supposed to respond? *Thanks? It's okay?*

It's not their fault my best friend died. It's not anybody's fault but the weather.

"Car accident. She passed away two years ago." I say because I know Chloe is wondering how Laura died.

When you tell someone that a person died, even if they don't know the person in the slightest, I think it's okay to tell them how they passed away. That's just my opinion.

I mean, come on. Everyone is always a little bit curious.

Chloe sighs. "Damn. Life's a bitch."

Life's a bitch. What an interesting response to say to someone who just said her best friend died.

But I admit, I agree with her. Chloe might be a killer, but she is right.

Life is a bitch.

1 4

After receiving a message back from Theo's friend, Benton last night, I am positive that Chloe is responsible for Theo, Devon, Ryan and Steven's disappearances.

I couldn't sleep after reading Benton's message. So, while Noah was sleeping, I decided to take the time to put all my evidence toward Chloe on my corkboard.

With the courtesy of social media, I downloaded and printed photos of Chloe, Steven, Theo, Devon and Ryan.

Then I tacked each of their photos on a small cork board that was once used for my work notes at my desk, along with each missing person's report.

Chloe's picture is tacked to the middle of the

board with the word: KILLER written in red sharpie on a post-it note under her smug grin.

And Noah just saw this whole damn thing.

I planned to move my board out of the house and into my truck before Noah woke up this morning, but he just walked into the living room. And he's staring right at it. *Too late to hide this now.*

"Ellie…" Noah stands behind our sofa, looking at the board that is now in my hands. "What is that?"

Once I heard his voice, I immediately turned my board around, but I know he saw what was on it.

"It's something that I was working on all night."

"What is it?" Noah raises his eyebrows.

I wish Benton messaged me back while Noah was still out of town instead of last night after I picked him up from the airport. Then I would have started this board sooner and Noah would have never seen it.

There is no sense in lying to my husband now. The board is in my hands even though it's turned around and Noah has perfect vision. He already saw this. There is no fooling him.

Reluctantly, I turn my new evidence board around to face Noah. He walks around the couch to sit down.

"Please don't tell me I need to see my therapist again," I say as soon as he takes first sight of Chloe and the men's photos.

"If you knew I was going to suggest that—"

"—I'm not losing my mind," I impatiently interrupt him. "Just look at everything and let me explain before you jump to conclusions."

"I'm the one that's jumping to conclusions. Okay…" he mutters, resting back against the cushions. "Go ahead. I'm listening."

I point to Devon, Ryan, Theo and Steven's photos. "These four men went missing at two places. Ghost Go-Go bar and Club fate."

Noah nods, still holding a blank expression.

I point to Ryan, then to Steven. "These two guys were at the Ghost bar on a Tuesday, the night they went missing. Not the same Tuesday night, but separate."

I move my finger across the board to Devon before touching Theo's photo. "And these two guys were at Club Fate the night they went missing. Devon was there on a Wednesday night."

I point to Chloe's photo. "Chloe works Tuesdays and Wednesdays at the Ghost Go-Go bar."

Noah's expression is still blank. It's taking everything in me to not be aggravated by his lack of emotion. I am not sure he understands what I am saying.

"Club Fate is only a block over from Ghost Go-Go bar, babe." Sighing, I cross my arms.

"Keep going." He points to Theo. "What about him? What day did he go missing?"

"I was getting to this guy." I move my finger across the board back to the picture of Theo. "This is Theo Dian. He was the last piece of the puzzle."

I go on to tell Noah that I found Theo's Facebook just as easily as it was for me to find everybody else who reported their friends or family missing.

"The power of the internet," Noah sighs, smiling.

"Exactly!" I smirk, happy to see somewhat of a response out of him. "So, I found out what happened with Theo the night he disappeared. Well, sort of. Theo lives in New York. He was in town visiting a friend for a wedding. I messaged his friend the other day and he got back to me last night. Want to hear what he said?" I ask with my phone in hand, ready to reiterate the message from Benton.

"Go ahead," Noah nods, still expressionless.

I go on to read the message from Benton. "Theo was in town for my wedding on April 15th. That was the last time I saw him in person, but then I talked to him on Friday, April 19th. He texted me, the night before his flight to go back home while he was at Club Fate downtown. I don't know if he went to another place after that or anywhere else that night. His mom called me on Saturday when he didn't get off his flight back in New York. Then we found out he never checked out of his hotel room. I already told the police all this. If you have any more questions, I'll do my best to answer but that's really all I know. I just hope he turns up soon. Thanks for your interest in his case."

When I am done reading the message, I look up from my phone and see Noah still staring at me.

"What did you say to that guy to get all that information?" Noah asks. "Did you tell him about Chloe?"

"No," I shake my head. "I told him that I was an upcoming crime blogger, and this was my first case. I'm investigating local disappearances."

To my surprise, my husband laughs.

"You're cute," he grins.

"Anyways…" I point to my board again.

"Look at these dates. Each person went missing within about a three week to one month timespan and they were all each seen at either two places: Club Fate and Ghost Go-Go bar."

Noah has redirected his gaze from me to the corkboard. He just let out a long exhale.

"Can you please say something?" I anxiously break the silence between us.

"You need to be careful messaging and calling random people you don't know, Ellie. I can't believe you stalked people—"

"—stop saying I'm a stalker," I grunt.

"Okay. I'm sorry. But you *found* the identities of people you don't know online, found their addresses and jobs. Then you showed up in person to talk to them. Not to mention you lied about working for some blog to get your answer. I'm surprised nobody asked to see it."

"That's what you got out of all this?" I drop my hands at my side, sighing.

"Well, I admit. You do make a good case," Noah shrugs, nodding at the board. "You've put some thought into everything."

"Thank you," I smile.

"But you can't do anything with this board."

"What do you mean?" I narrow my eyes.

"What are you going to do, Ellie? Take this board to the police?"

"Uh, yes... Yes. I plan to do exactly that." I rest my hands on my hips. "This should be enough evidence to take to the station. I need to show them how each of these men's disappearances connect to each other. And that connection is Chloe. I have Benton's message to show the police. I just need to get every other person that I spoke to and bring them to the station together. Between everyone's stories, and the connection that I have to Chloe, the police would have to open an investigation. You just said it yourself— You said I make a good case."

"Babe, they won't take you seriously." Noah shakes his head. "Ellie, I'm not doubting you, but I don't like what you've been doing lately. This is not good for your mental health."

He touches the photo of Chloe in the middle of my board. "You've been hanging out with this woman, and you seriously think she's a killer. Ellie, come on. You literally slept inside of her house... I thought you told me you dropped this."

I *really* wish I had time to hide my board before he woke up. I knew he wouldn't understand.

"I know," I sigh.

I grab the board and move it to the floor, resting it up against my desk. "I couldn't sleep last night so this is what I did. I won't do anything. You're right. I'm crazy. I get it."

"You're not crazy. I understand your way of thinking, but you can't just go to the police with this. If there's something going on with those men that disappeared, I'm sure the police have it handled."

Yeah, sure they do.

"Okay. You're probably right," I nod.

"I think you should stop hanging out with Chloe if you still have these thoughts about her."

"Alright, fine," I mutter as I head toward our kitchen.

"Why don't you give your therapist a call today?"

And there it is.

"No, I'm fine," I insist. "I'm going to make us some coffee."

I knew Noah would act this way and it's understandable.

But it's also not fair to me.

He can't let the past determine the present. Or the future.

I know what I did before, and I made a fool of myself.

But that time was different.

This time, I have real evidence. I am not relying on just a theory in my head based off what I thought I was seeing.

One person is involved in the disappearances of Theo, Ryan, Devon, and Steven.

And I believe it is the woman who is living across the street from me.

15

I have been checking the Avery Missing Persons database daily since I mistakenly let Noah see my board. I told him that he was right about me taking my theory too far and that I threw out the whole board.

But I didn't. I still plan to go to the police with it.

Just not yet. If I do this, I need to do it right and I need to be careful. I thought I had enough evidence toward Chloe to take to the police but maybe Noah is right. Maybe I need just a little bit more before I deem her a killer to the authorities.

That is why I am sitting at the Go-Go bar while Chloe and her two annoying friends work tonight. I still don't remember either of the women's names and I also still don't care that much to learn them. I just want to observe Chloe for just a little while longer.

But not too much longer though.

According to the pattern in disappearances, a new male should have been reported missing in Avery by now. But there hasn't been a new person listed in Avery's database since Steven Shang appeared which was a little over a month ago.

I need to figure out why Chloe went off her pattern before I make my next move.

Noah left for another work trip yesterday, so I used the *'can't sleep without my husband'* excuse to Chloe. *(Bored sad housewife problems, again.)* I told her that I thought it would be fun to sit at the bar and people watch instead of eating at a Waffle House or a Diner alone. Sitting at a bar eating wings at three o'clock in the morning seemed like a better idea. Merely because it's entertaining.

And since Chloe is my only friend, why not hang out at the place where she works, right?

Again, I am not lying entirely. It truly is difficult to sleep at night without Noah beside me in bed except that is obviously not the real reason why I am here. I am here to observe Chloe.

She is dressed just like the other cocktail waitresses, wearing black booty shorts sporting the name Ghost on the back, black fishnet tights, and a matching crop top. And right now, she's getting pretty close to a male customer who is sitting alone at a table.

His light blonde hair is pulled back in a low bun. Tan skin. I don't know his height since he is sitting down. But his fitted black T-shirt wraps tightly around his muscles. He's clearly in shape.

Two other guys who I suppose are his buddies just brought two women over to the table. He doesn't seem to mind since his eyes are locked on Chloe. She's leaning one hand on the table, her other hand holding the now empty tray that once held his drink.

This is the first time I have been inside of Ghost Go-Go bar. I think this place seems more like a club than a bar. The music is louder than expected and people are dancing in several areas of the floor. Others are just lingering, and watching, merely taking in the scenery from the tables. Cocktail waitresses, including Chloe, float the glistening black floor.

After an hour of enduring the music and denying men who only take the word *no* after hearing it nearly ten times, I decided to leave and go home.

The customer who Chloe was flirting with never stood up from his table before I left the bar, so I didn't get a chance to see how tall he was. But at least I got a good enough look at him though.

If he comes back to Chloe's house tonight, and if he turns up in the missing persons list, I will remember his face. Then I will have my proof and be able to tell the police what I saw.

That is, *if* he goes missing.

If he doesn't, then I need a new plan.

It's four-thirty in the morning now. I just got home from the bar and Chloe is not back yet. Her shift ends in half an hour.

While I wait for her to come home, I make myself a cup of coffee and relax on my couch. I have the blinds slightly drawn open enough to see when she gets home from the bar which should be in about an hour.

Even though I am nearly chugging the coffee, my eyelids are starting to get heavy.

I don't want to fall asleep but if I do, I can take comfort in knowing that my security camera views her entire property now.

Because Noah was adamant on not wanting to invade our neighbor's privacy when first installing the camera years ago, he angled it to only see our front porch, our driveway, our front yard and the street in front of our house; also, in front of Chloe's house. It just so happened that the camera ended up viewing part of Chloe's driveway because of the angle it's positioned at.

But not anymore. Now the camera has a wider view of everything. Now it is pointed right at Chloe's entire property, the street in between us, my driveway, and my porch.

Unlike Noah, I don't care about invading our neighbor's privacy. Especially Chloe's. I can see everything that I need to see now.

The security camera is set to record motion as usual, (I couldn't figure out the settings to get the camera to record all the time) but now that it has a wider view of her property, it should record the moment Chloe parks her Jeep in the driveway, steps out of the driver's side and when she walks into the front door of her house.

Along with whoever walks in and doesn't walk back out.

16

"ARE YOU FUCKING KIDDING ME?"

Angling my security camera to face Chloe's house did not help at all last night.

Chloe isn't on any of the recordings because it started storming shortly after I fell asleep in the living room. The rain fell so heavy, my camera didn't catch any movement besides seven seconds of her Jeep headlights pulling into the driveway. That was around five-thirty this morning.

In the next recording, I saw another car drive down the street about half an hour later right after the rain cleared up. The car didn't stop in front of her house to drop or pick anyone up though. They drove right by.

If it weren't raining, my camera would have caught the moment Chloe got out of her Jeep and walked up to her door. Except the rain blocked all of that last night.

So, I have no idea if Chloe brought a man home from the bar with her after I left.

It's a few minutes past ten o'clock in the morning already and her Jeep isn't in the driveway anymore. Today is Friday so I know that she already left to start her shift at Jack's.

I don't know how she works all night at one job, sleeps for about three or four hours, then goes to the next job. Especially at the age of thirty. It's a bit more doable when you're in your twenties.

Or maybe Chloe doesn't sleep during those hours, and she uses the time in between jobs to kill instead.

I shouldn't...

Except I can't help myself.

Before I can think about it, my feet are leading me out of the house, across the street toward Chloe's, and up her driveway.

But as I'm walking, I realize if anyone in this neighborhood has an interest in Chloe as much as I do, then there might be a possibility that someone else could be watching me. Either I am being paranoid or just paranoid enough.

To be safe, I knock on the door as if I am expecting Chloe to be home.

Walking directly around to the backyard without knocking on the front door first will look strange if anyone really is paying attention to me.

But as I think about it, Chloe's nearest neighbors aren't even home right now. The neighbors who live in the house to the left of hers, leave for work around seven o'clock in the morning. The neighbors on the right leave half an hour later.

But then my eyes take notice of the small apartment complex two houses down, where Jeff lives.

Chloe said they dated briefly, and he became clingy which I saw from my window.

I don't need to worry about Jeff right now though. He's not home. He's at his construction job as he usually is Friday mornings.

I proceed to walk around to the backyard of Chloe's house, disappearing around the corner and onto her back porch. Her sliding door is locked.

Pressing my forehead against the glass to look inside of the house, I knock twice.

Noah would disapprove of what I'm doing if he knew. Hell, he would disapprove of me moving the position of our security camera. I'm sure he'll notice when he comes home from his trip. He'll probably tell me to change the angle because it's illegal or not morally right to watch other people's property and I will simply tell him *okay.*

But of course, I have no plans to move the camera back to its original position until I get what I need. I don't want another man to go missing but I need more evidence.

If I go to the police now, I might make myself look…unstable, let's call it.

And I don't want that to happen again.

Especially since nobody new has appeared missing. If I am wrong about the pattern, I need something else to back up my theory.

"Hello?" I yell, peering through the glass and trying to slide it open.

Sadly, Chloe's gotten better with

remembering to keep her backdoor locked.

There is no sign of a guy anywhere in her house and nobody is answering as I knock.

Either Chloe came home from work alone this morning or the man who I saw her flirting with at the bar last night is dead in there.

Or maybe there's a different guy in there.

Or maybe she already buried him back here in these woods behind her yard.

I turn around to face the trees.

Chloe isn't piling bodies only a few feet away from her own home back there.

That's impossible.

That also wouldn't be such a smart move. She would bury her victims way deeper into the woods where they would be harder to find.

And I know she doesn't have the strength to walk out there and carry a dead body alone.

If I can't do it, she can't.

Not that I've tried. I am just using common sense and physics.

Killers like to believe they think rationally. I am thinking like a killer.

I think that I am thinking rationally.

There are only two rational options I can come back to:

Option A: Chloe drags the bodies out of the back door, through this backyard, and through the woods by herself on foot.

Given her height and weight, unlikely. She wouldn't have enough strength to get very far so she would have to opt for burying her victims close to her yard.

I leave her back porch and head straight into the woods.

A few feet in, I do not *see* any signs of burials or tracks in the dirt as I stand only a couple feet past the tree line bordering her yard and the woods.

Or

Option B: Chloe drives her Jeep through the front yard around to the backyard before she drags her victims through the sliding back door. Then she transports them out to the woods that way.

But there isn't any space for a vehicle to drive back here. The trees are too close together.

To transport her victims, she would need to drive outside of our neighborhood out to one of the roads that parallel the woods and find a dirt trail with access.

My only conclusion: I need to drive out into these woods myself to see if Option B could be possible.

Back home, from the back of my closet in my bedroom, I grab an orange hoodie and an old pair of boots that I haven't worn in years.

I rush back outside to get in my truck. Then I reverse back out of my driveway and head half a mile down the road toward the stop sign. I take a left down the road that parallels the woods behind Chloe's house.

About a thousand feet down, I spot the first dirt trail that tracks off the road. I am not the first person to come out here hence the previously created dirt trails. Other people presumably use these trails too. Hunters, teenagers, hikers… and probably killers. Probably Chloe.

Ten minutes of crawling my truck at a slow speed of five miles per hour, I brake at the end of the trail when it diminishes into a shorter dirt road that leads deeper into the woods. I continue to drive cautiously until I get about two-hundred feet down to the end. I step out of the driver's side and climb onto the bed of my truck so I can see from a taller view.

The houses in my neighborhood are not visible from out here, even as I stand on the bed of the truck. A person would have to walk through the woods on foot if they wanted to get back into my neighborhood. Not with a truck. Not even with an ATV.

I jump down from the bed of my truck. Then I set off on foot into the woods, leaving my truck at the end of the dirt road.

About six-hundred feet in, I still don't see any sign of my neighborhood. No houses in the distance. No human remains or traces of anyone being out here either.

And now I'm starting to hear noises. Either animals or leaves falling off the trees. Whatever it is, I don't want to find out.

This was impulsive, coming out here by myself in search of…well, I don't really know.

I need a better plan and a shower.

When I pull into my driveway a few minutes

later, and get out of the driver's side, I hear my name from across the street. "Ellie!"

Shit. It's Chloe.

Why isn't she still at work?

"Woah! Feeling in a bright mood today, huh?" Chloe walks up my driveway. She's talking about my orange sweatshirt which is a bit wet from my sweat.

"Yeah," I mumble while closing my truck door. "Aren't you working today?"

"Yeah, but I left my charger at home, so I came back for it." She looks down at my boots. "Where were you? I've never seen you dressed like this."

Looking for the dead bodies that you buried behind your backyard.

"I just went for a walk through the forest. I don't know," I shrug. "I decided I need some fresh air. I wore bright colors in case any hunters were out there. This was the brightest thing I had in my closet. I had nothing to do today. Noah gets home from his trip tomorrow."

Chloe remains still. Her expression portrays confusion, not surprise. She is not fidgeting. No paleness in her face. No sign of worry in her body movements or expression.

If she were burying men out in the woods, she would surely show a look of panic or something after I just mentioned I was roaming around out there for really no reason at all.

Unless she's just really that good at lying.

"Didn't you just drop him off the other day? His trips are short," Chloe remarks.

Again, she is being negative about my

husband's work schedule.

"Sometimes," I shrug.

"Well, call me next time you go on a hike! That sounds fun." Chloe turns slightly to look over toward her house. "I've never walked back through those woods. It sounds peaceful. I never thought about it."

"I needed a change of scenery." I say, acting as casual as Chloe is. "I'll see you later." I start to walk toward my front door when Chloe stops me.

"Oh, you coming by the bar tonight then? Since Noah's not home?"

"Most likely," I wave as I unlock my door and walk inside my house.

Instead of showering, I go sit at my desk and watch Chloe walk back to her house. I turn on my computer. Then I click on my online saved bookmark: **Avery Missing Persons.**

I let out a relieved breath when I see that Bianca, the teenager who I received an Amber Alert about in July, and the elderly man with dementia have both been found.

It is also a relief to see that nobody new is reported missing since Steven disappeared.

But at the same time, it's confusing.

Why isn't anybody new on this list?

I am starting to think that I either didn't identify the correct pattern in Avery's local disappearances and I am wrong…

Or I'm right. Which means Chloe might know that I'm on to her.

SEPTEMBER

17

September 9th

Wednesday

Malik Jenson. Age 31. 5'9. Reported missing by his girlfriend on September 8th.

This doesn't make any sense. It's been two months since Steven disappeared. The timing between each victim is off.

But when it comes to his physical description, Malik matches the rest of the missing men. He is in shape and tall; between the height of five foot eight inches to six feet tall, and he's in the same age range as the other victims.

And Malik went missing last night on a Tuesday.

But I was at the bar last night, or should I say, early this morning and I didn't see him.

Last night also happened to be the first time I went back to the Ghost bar since August when Noah went out of town. I wanted to go back to the bar since then, but I knew Noah would not believe me if I told him that my mind changed about Chloe being a killer. So while he was on his last work trip this year, I took my opportunity to observe Chloe last night.

But I swear that I didn't see Malik at the bar when I was there. I would recognize him from this photo if he and Chloe were flirting. And he was not one of her customers. At least, not in the few hours that I was there.

And Malik did not come home with Chloe this morning. I played back my camera footage after I picked Noah up from the airport this morning.

I left the bar around three in the morning, went home and showered. Then I left at five o'clock to pick Noah up. Chloe wasn't home yet when I drove by. She normally gets out of work at that time.

And by the time I got home from the airport with Noah, her Jeep was parked in the driveway. My camera footage only showed Chloe walk into her house alone.

Even though Noah just flew back home only four hours ago, he still needs to go into the office later this evening. So while he is at home resting from his flight before he goes back into the office later, I am going to find out more about Malik's disappearance. The description in his report doesn't state his whereabouts before his girlfriend reported him missing, which I find even more interesting.

Malik has a girlfriend, so I assume he was not at a bar or a club, flirting with other women or cocktail waitresses. Like I was told that Devon, Ryan,

Steven, and possibly Theo had all been doing before they went missing.

But I can only assume until I know the truth. Maybe Malik isn't such a good boyfriend. Maybe he was a cheater.

After doing an online search for the name: *Malik Jenson, age 31 in Avery, Florida,* I found his profile. Then I found his girlfriend.

IN A RELATIONSHIP WITH: Louisa Ramirez.

Louisa works at a restaurant that I have eaten once or twice at in town.

My first idea was to arrive at her job like I did with Henry but she wasn't working, so I left and just drove to her address.

I find it odd that it is easy to get a person's address by simply searching online, yet it's more challenging to find their phone numbers. I'd prefer to call, rather than show up and risk my safety as Noah nearly scolded me about, but an address is my next and only option.

I am turning off my engine in the driveway of Louisa's when my cell phone rings.

My husband. *Remember when I said a benefit of marriage is telepathy?*

"Hey, babe. Surprised you're not still sleeping," I answer.

"I just woke up. I was thinking we could go out for lunch when you get back. We haven't gone out to lunch in a while."

"Oh, I thought you told me you were going into the office this afternoon?"

"They can wait a day. I just got back. I'm too tired from my flight," Noah says through a yawn.

"Oh! Okay, that sounds good." I can't hide the shock in my tone. I am happy to hear that my husband finally said no to his job for once in nearly ten years, but I am not happy that he did it today.

I am too busy investigating Chloe.

"I'll be home in about an hour. I'm almost done shopping. Haven't found anything I want, really," I tell him, wincing as I hear myself lie.

"Can't wait. Love you." Noah's excited tone of voice makes me smile. And slightly tear up.

I want to be truthful with him. I really do.

"I'll see you when I get home. Love you."

If Noah knew that I am still friends with Chloe, he would get worried that I am still suspicious of her.

In that case, he would be right.

I get out of my truck and walk up to the black painted front door of Louisa's apartment on the first floor.

After knocking twice, a puffy red-faced woman answers the door.

"Hi. My name is Ellie," I say with a smile. "Sorry to bother you. I saw that your boyfriend Malik was reported missing. I had a few questions about what happened to him. If you don't mind, it will only take a few minutes."

"Were you the bitch he left me for last night?" Louisa straightens her torso, hands on her hips. Her defeated weakened state has turned defensive.

Shit. I was not expecting a confrontation.

"N—no." I stutter while flashing my wedding ring. "I'm married. Uh, I have been investigating missing men in the area, and I believe your boyfriend might fit a pattern in certain disappearances. I have a few questions if you don't mind. I am just trying to piece some information together. I might be able to help—"

"Who are you with? Are you a reporter or something?" She cuts me off from talking. "How did you know Malik is missing?"

"Kind of. Yes. Well, not a reporter, but I write for my own crime blog. I just started it. I have a hunch and just going off it. This is my first investigation," I say. "I saw Malik's photo in the local missing persons database. That's the reason why I'm here."

After my lie, thankfully it doesn't take any more convincing.

Within the next couple of minutes, I am sitting on the chair across from Louisa outside of her apartment door.

"So, what made you report Malik missing? You said he was with another woman?"

"We were out downtown with my friends last night. He was being an asshole like normal and we got into a fight," Louisa sighs as a few tears escape her eyes. She inhales to hold them back. "He started dancing with all these other women to make me jealous. I didn't care and just let him do whatever he wanted. I ignored him for the rest of the night. But then he didn't call me this morning, so I called him, and it went to voicemail. I went to his apartment. He wasn't there." She stops to take a breath.

"We always do this. We fight and cheat on each other and now he's missing… and I, I just don't know what to do. Part of me doesn't care but part of me does care, you know?"

Nodding, I force a supportive smile. "I

understand. Love is tough."

I think I'm getting good at this fake empathizing with people thing.

I have no clue what Louisa is going through because my relationship with Noah is not even remotely close to what she just described. And it never has been.

Not to sound judgmental, but her relationship sounds a bit toxic and complicated. The opposite of the meaning of love, if you ask me.

But then again, I guess everyone has different definitions for *love.* Mine just isn't that.

"Where were you guys at? What was the place called?"

Louisa sniffles. "The Ghost bar."

I shake my head, exhaling.

Just because I didn't see Malik at the bar, doesn't mean he wasn't there before I was. Or he could have got there right after I left which was around three o'clock in the morning. Chloe worked for another two hours after that.

"Why do you look like that? What's going on?" Louisa looks at me up and down, forehead wrinkled.

I might be getting better at fake emphasizing but not with hiding my facial expressions.

"Well, I think a few other guys went missing from that same bar, Ghost Go-Go," I admit.

Louisa looks at me like she is waiting for more of an explanation on my part.

When I don't return her wish, she drops her head a bit, eyes narrowed. "What are you saying?"

I grab my phone out from my purse to show her Chloe's photo. "Do you remember seeing this woman last night?"

"Hmm," Louisa mumbles, staring at my screen. "I think so. She looks familiar."

"She does?" I exclaim. "Was this one of the women that you saw Malik dancing with?"

Louisa squints, shaking her head. "I don't think so." She nods toward my phone. "That woman is a waitress there. Malik wasn't with any of the waitresses."

"Wait, so you do know her?" I repeat, gesturing toward Chloe's picture.

"Well, *no*. I don't know her. I've seen her at the bar before though. I go to the Ghost bar with my friends a lot. But I don't remember seeing her there last night. She wasn't the waitress who served us. It was another woman, a taller waitress."

"What time did you, Malik and your friends get to the bar?" I ask as I put my phone back inside my purse.

"We got there around midnight. Malik and I got into a fight around two in the morning. He left the bar a half hour later. I left with my friends about fifteen minutes after he did."

"Did you see Malik leave? Did he leave with another woman?" I ask, confused.

"I didn't see him leave myself, but my friend said she saw him leave the bar with someone."

"But he wasn't with the woman in the photo that I showed you, right? You're positive it wasn't her?" I ask her again.

Louisa nods. "Positive."

Chloe was definitely working at the Ghost bar in between the hours that Malik and Louisa were there. But Louisa doesn't recall seeing her.

Malik left at two-thirty in the morning, and I arrived a few minutes past three o'clock.

So, we all just missed each other.

But Chloe worked from midnight until five o'clock this morning and I know she was there all night.

And I know that Chloe didn't come home with anyone after work either. She pulled into her driveway at five-thirty in the morning. The timestamp is on my camera footage.

She got out of her jeep alone. Not with Malik. Not with anyone.

Then according to the timeframe and what Louisa just told me, Chloe can't be responsible for Malik's disappearance.

So, then who is?

18

Something I regretfully have not done until now is a deeper look into who Chloe really is.

Besides her social media presence, I never looked into Chloe's actual background.

Does she have any felonies or any criminal charges? Where did she live before she moved to Avery?

And who the hell is her ex-boyfriend, the drunken asshole who supposedly lived with her? The man who I never seen before.

I still don't know why she lied about living with a man when she first moved here, and I am certain that she lied.

'I've had bad experiences with men. If Noah ends up being like one of those guys, I'll be here for

you.'

Why can't I get Chloe's words out of my head? Who says that about a person's husband when they just met them?

"Try to have a good day today, babe." Noah breaks my thoughts about Chloe at the front door of our house as he leaves for the office.

He thinks I am working today but I requested a personal day instead.

I lock the front door after my husband leaves for work before pouring a glass of wine in my kitchen.

When I sit at my desk, I search online: *Chloe Jones in Avery, Florida. Age 30.*

Several people with the same name come up in the search results. But the fourth listing is the Chloe that I know. Or at least, I think I know.

When I click on the link to her name, I don't see anything alarming. No felonies or criminal charges. No public court records. She isn't on a list of sexual offenders either. Not that I thought she would be, but it doesn't hurt to check.

Although, I do see three addresses that are publicly listed under her name.

The first one being her current address; the house that is across the street from mine.

Last year, she lived in Kennesaw, Georgia.

And the year before that, she lived in Atlanta, Georgia.

Chloe has never mentioned living outside of Florida to me.

Then again, the topic of conversation has never been brought up either. I never asked Chloe where she moved from. I didn't even ask her why she moved here. I should have.

Maybe I still can.

I click off of the website that gives me all of this information so I can go back to Google Images under her name.

The first page of results shows multiple photos of other women that are not Chloe until I spot her Facebook profile image in the middle of the page.

Since I already know that her profile is private, I scroll past the profile image until Chloe's face catches my eye further down the list.

Then I see her again in another photo.

And again, in another.

In one photo, Chloe is posing next to a guy I've never seen before.

It looks like they were at a party or a club when they took this picture because people are crowded behind them in the background and drinks are in everyone's hands.

Clicking on the picture, it links me to the man's Facebook. His name is Terrance. He lives here in the town of Avery, and this picture with Chloe was posted last year.

No comments. Only ten likes. Chloe isn't tagged and she is not in his friends list either.

Scrolling through Terrance's profile, I see that he hasn't been active on it in months because his last post was about three months ago. I assume he might be one of Chloe's ex-boyfriends; Possibly the drunken ex-boyfriend that supposedly moved in across the street with her?

He looks like a drunk to me.

I click back over to the image results under *Chloe Jones* to view the other two photos.

In both photos, a different man is photographed with her. Shoulder length, thin brunette curls round his face. He is a few inches taller than Chloe. Tattoos cover both of his muscular arms, barely leaving any visible skin to be seen beneath the colored ink. *Again, someone I have never seen before.*

In one picture, they are sitting together in a car while the other photo shows them standing by a waterfall.

The first photo I click on links me to his social media profile. His name is *Jarod Stinger.* He posted this photo with Chloe about three years ago. Twenty-two likes but the comments aren't visible.

I swipe away to view his profile where it shows his name and age: *Jarod Stinger. Age 28.*

And then I see that he died three years ago in Atlanta, Georgia— the same year Google says Chloe lived there.

19

S e p t e m b e r 1 0 ^{t h}
T h u r s d a y

When I type *Jarod Stinger* and the date of his death into the search bar of Google, a page of results shows.

But only one website links me to the information that I need.

The headline on an article from a News Station in Atlanta, Georgia reads:

MAN STABBED TO DEATH IN DOMESTIC DISPUTE.

Police are investigating after a man, identified as Jarod Stinger, was found fatally stabbed in his residence at a condo complex on January 12th.

Police and paramedics were called to the condo complex at 4:02 a.m. where Jarod Stinger was found stabbed in the kitchen and assaulted over the head. He was pronounced dead at the scene.

Officials say a woman who remains unidentified, made the 911 call at the residence. She stated that she and Jarod got into an altercation. She was detained and later taken for evaluation.

Police are still investigating.

This isn't a coincidence. Chloe is a killer. I fucking knew it.

20

September 10th
Thursday

"You killed him!" My feet have taken over everything in me. I jogged over to Chloe's house and banged on her front door just now.

Once she opened it, I pushed my way right past her and into her living room with my evidence board in hand.

Which I had been hiding my board under the enclosed cover in the bed of my pickup truck ever since I told Noah that I would get rid of it.

I plan to confront Chloe with the face of each man on here. She's going to confess, and I will record it all on my phone. Then I'll call the police, and nobody will be able to call me crazy. Not after I give them her recorded confession.

I already opened my camera app and put the

phone in the pocket of my jean shorts. She won't have any idea that I'm recording her.

"Wh--what?" Chloe's face has turned pale. She's frozen by the kitchen counter.

"You're a killer!" My feet are still moving faster than my mind is.

"What are you talking about?" Chloe stutters.

"I know about Jarod! He's dead!" I say through my teeth, fists at my side as I back closer toward the sliding glass door. "You killed him!"

Where is the nearest weapon in this house? Why didn't I grab something useful to defend myself before running over here?

There aren't any knives out on the kitchen counter. Not that I am close to the kitchen anyways.

Nothing sharp in front of me on the living room table…

I only spot an umbrella next to the backdoor that's leaning on the wall, a few steps away from my feet.

Guess it will have to do. I drop the board at my feet as I step back to grab the umbrella and raise it toward her. "Stay there!"

"Ellie, what the hell are you doing with that?" Chloe shakes her head, eyes narrowed. "Put the umbrella down! You can't hurt me with that! What the hell is going—"

"Answer me!" I interrupt, shouting with the umbrella aimed at Chloe.

"Jarod is one of my ex-boyfriend's, Ellie! He attacked me, and I defended myself. I told you about him. I told you that I had an ex who physically abused me. Please, Ellie… I don't understand why you're here…"

"So, you killed him, right?" I yell.

"You killed Jarod. Admit it!"

"Ellie… I—," she stutters. "Yes. I did. But it was out of *self-defense*. He used to abuse me. Multiple times. One day, he was hitting me, and I just, I—I knew that it was going to be him or me in that moment. I had to do it. I couldn't take his abuse anymore." Chloe's staring at me with teary eyes. "How did you find out about him?"

I am not sure if she is lying.

She's not crossing her legs. She isn't fidgeting. She's looking right at me.

The Atlanta news report never said who stabbed Jarod. Although it implied that a woman was at the scene because the report stated she got detained, then taken for an evaluation. The headline also stated a man was stabbed in a domestic dispute.

But maybe it wasn't actually a domestic dispute.

"Internet," I say through my teeth. I back up and bend at my knees slightly to pick up the corkboard. I toss it onto the sofa that is in between us.

"Explain all those men!" I demand, pointing at the board. "You're a killer and a liar!"

Chloe hesitates before stepping closer to the couch. Her eyes widen when she sees her own photo tacked in the middle of the board. "Ellie, you need to take a deep breath. Why is my picture here? I don't know what you're—"

It is when I see Chloe's eyes lock onto Malik's picture, and she suddenly stops talking. Her forehead creases. Her head tilts just slightly to the left.

She's looking right at him.

"I… I know him," Chloe shakes her head. "Well. No, I don't know him *know him*. Wait… He's missing?"

Glaring at her, I remain silent.

Chloe briefly looks at me, then points to Malik. "I saw him leave the Go-Go bar with Theresa the other night. She was all over this guy. You were at the bar that same night too."

Chloe looks back to the board before she touches Ryan's photo, her eyes growing wider. "Holy shit…" She murmurs, shaking her head. "Ellie, you have to explain all of this to me. I'm not responsible for these missing men, but I think I might know who could be."

21

"Start talking." I have allowed Chloe to sit on the couch while I stand in front of the chair next to her in the living room. I still have the umbrella grasped tightly in my hand.

"I saw Theresa flirting with Malik at work. He was at the bar earlier in the night, but then I saw him outside near her SUV when I was walking to my car after my shift. I think he went home with her after her shift ended."

My eyes narrow. "Who the hell is Theresa?"

Chloe draws her head back, giving me a perplexed look. "We hung out with her. You know… Theresa and Gianna? Those are the women that work with me at the bar. The four of us hung out downtown." She tilts her head. "You've even said hello to them the few times you been at the bar…" Chloe lets her words trail off, her expression increasing with perplexity.

So that was their names. Theresa and Gianna were the two women in their early twenties that Chloe forced me to hang out with.

"Which one was Theresa?" I try to picture both women. The blonde was taller, and the brunette was shorter. That's really all I remember.

"Theresa left early that night. Gianna hung out with us the rest of the time…" Chloe answers, still holding a look of confusion. "You never knew their names?"

I ignore her question and ask my own. "What are you trying to tell me about Theresa?"

Chloe touches the words *Club Fate* that I wrote in red Sharpie on Ryan's report. She moves her finger over to *Club Fate* written in red under Theo's photo. "Theresa works at Club Fate too."

I don't know how to read this woman right now. Chloe isn't fidgeting. No hesitation. She's not crossing her legs. Even though her attention is divided between me and the photos on the board, she looks completely stunned — like she's not faking her reaction.

Unless she is faking it so well, her reaction is almost believable.

Chloe probably planned to tell this lie. She was prepared to be confronted one day, whether it was going to be by me or by somebody else. I bet she is just trying to put the blame on another person. Somebody that I know. Somebody who works at the bar with her. She can't fool me.

Chloe looks at her photo on the board. I have

bullet points written underneath her picture:

- Guys walk in her house but never leave
- Finding victims at Club Fate and Ghost Go-Go bar
- Ghost bar work schedule: Tues/Wed/Thurs
- Days men went missing (except Theo): Tuesday and Wednesday

"My face shouldn't be here." Chloe looks at me. "Theresa works at the Ghost bar Tuesday, Thursday, and I think Sunday nights. But I don't know what her schedule is at Club Fate."

My expression remains blank, prompting Chloe to gesture toward Ryan's photo. "I'm pretty sure that I've seen this guy at the bar too. I think Ryan and Malik are both regulars. They've come in a few times. Not together…" Her words drag.

How coincidental. Ryan's sister didn't recognize Chloe and neither did Sherry's husband. If they were regular customers at the Ghost bar, they would have recognized Chloe when I showed them her picture. Just like Malik's girlfriend did.

Unless Ryan only went to the bar often and Sherry and her husband don't.

I remember Sherry telling me they were celebrating her new promotion with her brother that night. Maybe Ryan chose the bar to celebrate at.

I remain quiet, staring at Chloe as I contemplate her words. She still hasn't told me exactly what happened between her and Jarod yet. The news report alluded to a domestic dispute involving a woman. But just because the police report says it was domestic violence, how do I know if that story is true?

"Show me proof that you killed Jarod out of self-defense." I glare at her.

Chloe scoffs, like she is in disbelief that I am asking such a question. "If you need proof, then I need to get my phone in my bedroom. I need to show you a Facebook post."

Like hell you're leaving this room or leaving my sight.

"We can use mine," I respond firmly.

"Fine." Chloe exhales. "Go on Facebook. Search the name Adrianna Lynn in Atlanta, Georgia."

When I reach for my phone in my jean pocket, it reminds me that the camera app has been recording. If I swipe away to go on Facebook, my phone will stop recording...

But I am not letting her move from that couch. I don't trust her.

With my eyes partially on Chloe, I end the camera recording and swipe away to go on Facebook.

Eleven search results show up under the name *Adrianna Lynn. Atlanta, Georgia.*

"What am I looking for?"

"If you give me your phone, I'll show you." Chloe crosses her arms while remaining seated on the couch.

I hesitate briefly before I toss my phone toward her, still managing to keep about two umbrella lengths of distance between us. Not close enough for her to yank it out of my hand, and not far enough away that I can't strike her with it.

After a few seconds of scrolling and clicking on my screen, she tosses the phone back to me. It lands on the chair beside me. When I pick it up, I see a photo of Jarod with another woman who I assume is Adrianna.

"Read what the post says and the comment thread under it," Chloe sighs.

My eyes divert to the caption written by Adrianna.

I know that my brother wasn't perfect. I wish the situation in his passing was in better circumstances. I wish he could have gotten help with his issues.

I also wish Chloe asked for help too. Maybe if she spoken out about my brother's abuse toward her, then both Chloe and Jarod would be in different situations right now. At least, Jarod would be alive.

I miss you so much, bro. I love you.

There are five hundred and sixty comments underneath the post. Several people offer condolences to Adrianna while other comments are from people who are skeptical of the way Jarod died.

I don't believe that bullshit. She didn't have to kill him.

He is watching over you, Adrianna.

I miss you, man. Regardless of what they say, you didn't deserve to die.

But as I keep scrolling, I also see quite a few comments against Jarod. Some people believe Chloe's self-defense story to be true.

Jarod was an asshole and an abuser. This

isn't shocking to hear. Sorry Adri.

She did what she had to do.

She did speak up. No one listened.

Did she really have to kill him, though? Did it have to get that far?

She wasn't so nice to him, either. Not from what he told me.

Chloe did tell me that one of her ex-boyfriends was abusive toward her, but she never said who… *"One of my ex's not only cheated on me once but three times. The guy after him beat the shit out of me and the guy after that became a lazy drunk that couldn't pay the bills."*

I have spent all my time learning about Chloe's routine and who she is now, but I never thought twice about the person she was or could have been before she moved across the street from me.

Along with the News headline of a Domestic Dispute, Adrianna's Facebook post coincides with Chloe's self-defense story…

But still, my eyes lock on to the comments that are skeptical of Jarod's passing.

"I have a copy of the police report in my room. If you let me get it, I'll show you," Chloe says.

I debate my options. I can't let her out of my sight. But I want to see the police report.

I *need* to see the police report.

Gesturing toward the hallway with the umbrella, I nod. "Get up but walk slowly."

22

September 10th
Thursday

With her palms out to her sides, Chloe walks slowly toward the hallway. I follow a foot behind her as I scan the house for anything better than this damn umbrella.

Nothing.

We get to her bedroom door which is already slightly open. She walks in first while I remain at the doorway.

I watch her begin to open a drawer from her dresser.

"Slowly," I say as she reaches her hands in the drawer.

Slowing her arm movements and rolling her eyes, Chloe pulls out a binder, opens it and holds a piece of paper out toward me.

I snatch it out of her hands quickly before stepping back against the doorframe, umbrella still raised.

ATLANTA, GEORGIA POLICE REPORT.
Date: 1/12/2020
Domestic Violence and Assault
Time 4:02 a.m.

My eyes skim past all the jargon in the report until I see the case description and the notes that are written by the Police officer who arrived at the scene first.

Officer Wheeler's notes:
At approximately 4:02 a.m. I responded to a 9-1-1 call where a woman told the operator that she reacted to a fight with her boyfriend, Jarod Stinger by stabbing him during a physical altercation.
Jarod Stinger was found fatally stabbed in the stomach once, assaulted in the head, and lying on the floor in the kitchen of their condo complex when I arrived.
Chloe Jones was fully cooperative and answered all questions.
She was detained at the scene, then taken for further mental and physical evaluation. Previous calls for domestic disputes have been reported to this address.
This case is marked as a self-defense case.

"Tell me what happened in your words." I

hand the paper back to Chloe.

She inhales sharply and sits on the edge of her bed. "Jarod abused me for a long time. That night it happened; he pushed me into the wall. He grabbed my hair, punched me in my stomach, and we fought. I got away and ran to the kitchen, grabbed a knife out of the drawer and when I turned around, he was coming right at me. That's when I stabbed him in the stomach. Then I grabbed the toaster off the counter and slammed him over the head with it."

The way Chloe delivers her story sounds as if it is a rehearsed lie, like she's repeated it many times.

Or she's telling the truth and she can't get the moment out of her head.

Something that traumatizing *would* be hard to forget.

"And that's how you killed Jarod?" I look her up and down.

"And that's how I defended myself." Chloe stands up from the bed, crossing her arms at her torso.

"I didn't call 9-1-1 right away. It took me a few minutes to call after it happened because I couldn't think straight. Jarod bled out too long and that's how he died. If I called for help a few minutes sooner, maybe Jarod would have lived, but he didn't." She exhales. "I had to do what I did. You don't understand. I went through years of abuse with that man. And I'm not sorry for what I had to do to stop it. Did you befriend me this whole time because you were investigating me?"

Obviously yes but we'll get to that later.

"Why haven't I ever seen any of your male guests leave this house then? Explain that."

"W--what?" Chloe draws her head back, scrunching her forehead.

"I've seen you invite different guys over here, but they never leave your house. What did you do with them?"

Chloe's expression has turned into a look of amusement. "Do with them? What do you think we did?"

I am about to slap her over the head with this damn umbrella.

"I meant, why haven't I ever seen anybody leave here?" I demand through gritted teeth. "My security camera has proof that no man has ever walked out of this house after walking in through your front door." I point toward her hallway, gesturing to the front of the house.

"So that's why you asked me about Colby a while back," Chloe mutters as she sits back down on her bed.

"Colby?" I shake my head. *Now I am getting angry.* "Who the hell is Colby?"

"That's who you saw at my house a few months ago when we first started hanging out – when you asked me if I was dating anyone." Chloe creases her eyebrows.

I thought I saw Steven Shang walk into her house that night.

Okay. I speculated that was who I saw.

"Well, then I never saw *Colby* leave the next day. Explain why."

"I--I don't know what to say to you, Ellie," Chloe lets her words linger, confusion growing over her expression. "When I have company, I tell the guy to leave before the sun rises. I don't want them to stay over here too long. They normally get a ride from a friend, or they take an Uber back home early morning."

I remain quiet. *That doesn't answer my question.*

After a moment, Chloe tilts her head. "Ellie, can your camera see everything outside? Does it see my whole front yard?"

My camera sees everything now.

However, it didn't before a month ago. Where is she going with this?

"Why are you asking?" I glare at her.

"Because whenever I invite a guy over, which hasn't been often by the way," Chloe scrunches her forehead. "I always tell the man to have their ride pick them up on the street toward the left side of my house; The opposite way from where Jeff lives. I know he wakes up early for work and like I told you before, he got kind of clingy after we had a few dates. I don't want him in my business," she sighs. "If your camera can't see that far onto the street, then that's probably why it hasn't caught any of my *guests* leave." She says '*guests*' condescendingly. "They don't walk down my driveway. They just leave through the front door and walk down the left of my yard toward the road."

Before I moved my security camera to view Chloe's entire property, it was only pointed toward my front yard, my driveway, the street in between our houses and just enough of Chloe's driveway to see when she got in and out of her Jeep.

If a person walked out of her front door and down the yard toward the left side of the road in those months before I moved the angle of my camera,

I don't think it would have recorded the moment each man left.

Not if each person didn't walk down the middle of her driveway like Chloe is telling me they didn't…

And if Chloe's story about Jarod is true, which seemingly it is, that means she probably doesn't want to draw attention to herself. That's why she covers her work uniform, so that nobody is in her business, like Jeff.

She has an explanation for almost everything except for her two friends that I never thought twice about: Theresa and Gianna.

Especially Theresa.

"Aren't you best friends with Theresa and Gianna?"

Chloe shakes her head. "Not at all. I only get drinks with them outside of work occasionally. Theresa invited me to get drinks with them so I thought I would invite you that night."

"Why did you ask me to hang out with them if you're not so friendly with either of those women then?"

"Because you were the one who asked me to get drinks in the first place. Remember, you invited me out on a Tuesday night because Noah was working late? You said you didn't want to go to a club, but you hadn't gone out in a while. I said I couldn't go out because I was working." Chloe looks away and for a moment, I think I see a look of genuine hurt on her face. "That's why I asked you to come hang out with Theresa and Gianna when they invited me. I thought you and I were becoming friends."

As I think about my investigation into Chloe over the past few months, I realize now that I never saw her around Theresa or Gianna besides the night that I was with the three of them.

Actually… no one went into Chloe's house during these past few months besides the guy I saw around the time of Steven's disappearance. The guy who Chloe said was named Colby.

Thinking about it now, I never saw Chloe go anywhere besides her house, Jack's Market and the Go-Go bar.

Still, skepticism holds over me.

I won't let three months of investigating Chloe end so easily.

"I need to talk to Theresa myself," I say.

"Then come to the bar tonight. Theresa's scheduled to work the same shift as me," Chloe says. "You can confront her yourself. You can ask her whatever questions you want to ask her."

"What is Theresa's username?" I pull my phone back out of my pocket. "Show me her profile."

"She's not on social media. At least, not that I know of. She's never mentioned it. I told you, we're not really that close," Chloe exhales, rolling her eyes.

"What's Theresa's last name?"

"I have no idea."

Of course, you don't.

"Isn't it on an employee schedule or something? Can't you get it that way?"

"Our schedule only shows first names. I can ask her what her last name is tonight." Chloe raises her eyebrow. "Or you can ask her yourself."

I think that's my only option.

I have the upper hand now. Until Chloe leaves

for her shift at the bar tonight, I will be watching her from inside of my house through the window.

I am confident that she will not call the police on me because there is nothing to call the police about. What is she going to say? That I accused her of murder? With what evidence?

"As soon as you pull out of your driveway tonight, I'll be following." I walk out of the hallway and grab my evidence board before heading toward the front door.

2 3

September 11th
Friday

12:00 a.m.

Since Noah has no more business trips left to go on this year, I had to lie to him tonight.

This time, I had no choice but to go with my only option: Telling him that I want to be friends with Chloe and all my thoughts about her being a killer have left my mind. And I am serious this time.

"My imagination had got the best of me. I promise I won't let it happen again. It's good that I realized it before I went overboard this time, babe. Chloe is actually a nice woman and friend. I let my crazy imagination take over," I had said to Noah which he in turn, responded, *"You're not crazy, babe."*

I ignored his sweet comment and continued by saying, *"The board I made is gone. You were right. I'm sure the police have it handled, and Chloe isn't the suspect."*

Then I further convinced him when I said Chloe invited me to go out with her and two of her friends for drinks tonight, so that is where I will be.

Technically, I wasn't entirely lying to my husband this time. Chloe did invite me to the bar with her friends. Noah just doesn't know that Chloe and her friends are working tonight, and now I am suspicious of all three of them.

"You see her right there? Long curly blonde wig. Red heels." Chloe nods across the bar towards Theresa who is serving a tray of drinks to a table.

Theresa is a tall woman, about five foot eight, with a toned frame of body.

But still, she doesn't look strong enough to lift a dead body, let alone a six-foot-tall male.

She's wearing ankle high red heels, black fishnet tights, black booty shorts sporting *Ghost Go-Go* with a white ghost across the back and a matching black crop top.

"The curly blond ponytail? That's a wig?" I raise my eyebrows, staring at Theresa's dirty blonde curly hair that is styled up in a high ponytail.

I do remember Theresa having blonde hair the night I met her.

Ryan's sister said the woman that Ryan left the bar with had long blonde hair.

If Theresa takes her hair out of the ponytail she's wearing now, her hair will probably fall past her hips.

"Didn't you ever notice that Theresa's hair

looks different? She always wears wigs," Chloe says.

No, I did not notice that because I was too busy paying attention to you. Not anyone else.

"Does Theresa ever wear black wigs?"

Adam, Devon's friend told me; The woman that Devon left with wore a lot of makeup and had short black hair.

"Maybe," Chloe shrugs. "She wears different styled wigs."

Every person that I spoke with described a different description of the woman each missing man was last seen with.

But maybe they were describing the same woman… just disguised in different appearances.

Comparing Theresa to Chloe as I look at both women now, I notice they are physically and when it comes to their looks, very different from each other. Theresa is at least two or three inches taller than Chloe with heels on. Chloe wears barely any makeup while Theresa is wearing tons of it. I can see dark rouge on her cheeks and black eye shadow covering her eyelids from about a hundred feet away in a dark bar. Burgundy red lipstick, perfectly stenciled in eyebrows, black winged eyeliner. It is obvious Theresa contours her makeup. And unlike Theresa, Chloe has naturally pale skin with and without foundation.

"What color is Theresa's real hair?"

"I don't even know." Chloe shrugs. "That's if she even has any," Chloe exchanges her glance over toward Theresa. "She shows up at the bar already dressed in her cocktail outfit. She's the only one who does that here. Everyone else gets dressed in the fitting rooms before our shift starts."

"What about Gianna?" I ask, scanning the bar to look for her.

"What about her?" Chloe creases her eyebrows. "I don't know what that woman knows about Theresa."

Of course you don't.

I turn my back toward Chloe to keep looking for Gianna when Chloe taps my shoulder.

"She's right there. Black tights. Short blonde curls," Chloe says, nodding toward the left of us.

Gianna is roughly mine or Chloe's height. Brunette shoulder length curls round her face. She wears the same black crop top and shorts that match the rest of the cocktail waitresses.

And since I am idiotically looking right at her, I just caught her attention. She's heading right toward us.

"Hey girl! Nice to see you here again!"

And now she's right in front of me. Great.

Gianna hugs me and I fight the urge to cringe, reluctantly wrapping my arms around her back.

Chloe was right. I've greeted her and Theresa here in the bar when I was secretly watching Chloe a few times. But again, I only briefly greeted and proceeded to forget about them.

"Table ten are assholes. They better tip me good." Gianna complains to Chloe before walking away and toward the kitchen behind the bar.

Before coming to the bar, I searched for Theresa through Chloe's followers and friends on her social media despite what Chloe said.

Knowing it was a shot in the dark without a last name, I even tried to search online with just the name *Theresa, Avery, Florida, Ghost Go-Go,* and

Club Fate.

And it was a shot in the dark. I didn't find a thing about her.

But I did find Gianna's profile after clicking on almost all of Chloe's two hundred and two followers.

Gianna's content consisted of photos of her working here at the Ghost bar and a lot of useless selfies. In some photos, she had on a uniform which I assume is for another bar or restaurant that she works at. I just don't know the name because Gianna did not tag the place in any of her posts and her uniform is only an apron with black shorts with a black collared shirt beneath it.

But Gianna does have a lot of friends. No, Theresa was obviously not one of them, but I found it weird that she wasn't pictured in any of Gianna's photos. She wasn't in any tagged photos either.

So as far as Gianna goes, I am not sure if she is helping Theresa or even knows about what Theresa is doing.

That is, if Theresa is doing what I thought Chloe was doing.

The only thing I am certain of; there is a killer here in Avery and it is either Theresa or Chloe.

But Chloe has an explanation for everything, and I am not sure how I feel about it.

I realized that every time I saw Chloe invite a guy over, she arrived home at night... before sunrise. She couldn't have brought any of those guys home from the Ghost bar because she works from midnight until five in the morning. The sun is usually about to rise as she is getting home.

And as far as showing traits of being a liar

toward me, technically Chloe is. She holds a secret.

Her past with not only Jarod but the other shitty men she described being with, they all traumatized her. That is probably what makes her personality give off certain liar traits. She likes to keep her guard up, to keep herself safe.

The news report about Jarod's death, the police report that Chloe showed me, and Adrianna's post about her brother on social media backs up Chloe's story.

If I see proof, I have to believe it.

But how do I believe Theresa is my new suspect now?

I need more than an absence of an online presence, wigs and Chloe's word to believe it.

Throughout the next two hours, I split my attention between Theresa, Chloe and Gianna as they walk from table to table across the dimly lit bar.

Gianna looks like she is just trying to get through the night. Giving casual smiles to each customer, occasional complaints to Chloe and Theresa. It doesn't seem like she even tries that hard to get a tip. No flirting with customers. No small talk.

Chloe seems like she is also just trying to get through the night. I notice she flirts with her customers more than Gianna does, but Theresa however, she really puts in the effort to get a nice tip. I watch her lean over the table, touch the customers arms, and laugh loudly.

And she is especially friendly with the taller, athletic body type in males. Men who look to be in their mid-twenties to early thirties. Men who have similar physical attributes to the five men who have

SARA KATE

went missing here in Avery.

OCTOBER

24

I have spent many nights watching Chloe, Theresa, and Gianna at Ghost Go-Go bar over the past three weeks.

That also includes many nights of lying to my husband so that I can be at the bar without him figuring out my true motive.

In time, I will tell him the truth. For now, my secret stays between me and Chloe.

It wasn't until I saw the traits in what I looked for in Chloe that started to show in Theresa when I decided that Theresa is my new suspect.

A not so clear, but doable enough image of Theresa (courtesy of a photo that I snuck of her at the bar since there is zero proof of the woman on the internet) now replaces Chloe's photo on my evidence board.

After countless nights of watching Theresa, I have noticed that she does wear wigs, just like Chloe told me she does. Theresa has worn a range of different styles and colors, except I have yet to see her wear a black short wig. Like how Devon's friend, Adam described the woman who he saw him with before he disappeared.

"You watching?" Chloe walks over to me from behind the bar.

"I am." I sip my drink, my body slightly turned to the left to see Theresa.

She stands beside a male customer at a table in the corner of the bar. She's smiling and touching his arm. Empty drinks at the table show that he had company, but they are no longer with him.

He just handed Theresa some cash and she pocketed the bills in her apron that she wears on the side of her left leg.

I watch the guy take his phone out of the pocket of his pants. She's leaning over his shoulder, saying something as he types on his phone.

It looks like she just gave him her number.

They're nodding and smiling.

She just kissed him on the cheek.

This is the first time I have seen Theresa act this way with a customer. She's been handsy and pretty flirty before, but I have yet to see her kiss someone.

Now he is starting to walk away from the table toward the exit of the bar.

"He's leaving. I wonder if he's going to meet up with her tonight," Chloe says, watching the encounter with me.

"Guess were going to find out." I get up from my barstool, leaving the money for my wine under the glass for the bartender.

"I'll see you out there." Chloe nods and I shuffle through the crowded bar, passing Theresa who I am trying to avoid before she can notice me.

But too late.

"Hey! You leaving already?"

The guy is almost out of my sight. If he weren't so tall, I wouldn't be able to still see him through the crowd.

"Yeah. I'm tired. I'll see you later." I try to push pass her, but she stops to give me a hug.

Noah would be so angry at me if he knew I am hugging a potential serial killer.

I break from her grip, fake a smile, and practically run through the crowd to get through the front door. The guy was walking in this direction. I assume he is already outside. I push past a couple who are dancing together and also very much in my way, and finally I'm out of the door.

But once I'm outside in the small parking lot in front of the bar, I don't see him anymore. He isn't near any of the cars parked outside of Ghost go-go either.

Maybe he crossed the street to another bar or club already.

My idea was to follow him to see where he was going. I might have even asked him if Theresa gave him his phone number just now, if they had plans to meet later.

Too fucking late for that now.

Shit… I wonder if Theresa knew what I was doing: that I was following him?

Is that why she stopped to give me a hug? So that the guy can get away from me?

Did she know I was following him?

That *was* a little odd how she abruptly stopped me when I was clearly in a rush to leave. Literally, I was practically jogging toward the exit.

In hindsight, that wasn't so smart of me.

Theresa hugged me the night we first met, (it was awkward then just as it was tonight) but never in the times I have been at the bar. She's only said a few words to me.

Why would she hug me and stop to say goodbye to me tonight?

What if it is because Theresa knew why I was in a rush? Maybe she knew I was going to follow that guy… She knew I was watching her all night.

What if I wasn't being as inconspicuous as I thought I was being during these past few weeks?

No. I'm overthinking this.

Theresa has no idea that I am suspicious of her because how could she know?

Chloe.

What if Chloe told her?

I can't watch Chloe twenty-four hours a day and I haven't been at the bar every night she works since I deemed her a killer to her face.

She's had plenty of time to tell Theresa my thoughts of her…

But why would she?

Although Chloe's explanations and self-defense story checked out, how can I trust her?

And why would she trust me?

I called her a fucking serial killer…

Well, I can't go back inside the bar since I

just told Theresa I was leaving for the night. If she spots me, that will look strange.

And if she isn't suspicious of me already, I will not let her become it.

I'll have to wait in my truck for Chloe's shift to end, which now I'm starting to wonder if I made a mistake trusting Chloe so soon.

I have allowed Chloe to stake out Theresa in the parking lot with me over the past few weeks now. She is supposed to meet me in my truck in three hours when her shift ends.

But did I let my guard down too early?

Or am I overthinking this whole situation?

25

October 8th
Thursday

As Chloe gets in the passenger side of my truck, Noah texts me.

Are you still out at the bar or heading back home yet?

Shit. It's five o'clock in the morning already. He's going to expect I come home soon. I know he's surprised I'm not back already. This is the latest I have been gone in a night. I normally come home by at least three in the morning when I tell him that I am hanging out with Chloe.

But I need an excuse to prolong my night out right now. Or my morning, I should say.

I'm at Chloe's friends, Theresa's. Sobering up with some coffee. Took an Uber here and taking one back to the bar to get my truck, then coming home. Don't worry. Love you!

Hitting send, my stomach flips. I have been lying to my husband too many times to count in these past few months.

Sighing, I put my phone in the cupholder between me and Chloe. "Noah's worried."

"That's so cute that he checks on you," Chloe remarks as she puts on her seatbelt.

"And here I am being a bad wife, lying to him." Unexpectedly, I feel tears escape my eyes. I inhale a deep breath. This is not the time for emotions.

"What do you mean, lying to him?" Chloe asks.

"Well…" I hesitate.

Chloe's told me her truth, but I haven't told her mine. I guess after everything, it's only fair.

"Noah doesn't know that we're watching Theresa. He thinks that I'm just having drinks with you two at the bar."

"Oh…" Chloe nods, still holding a look of confusion.

"I told Noah that I thought you were a killer months ago and he told me to call my therapist," I exhale.

"*Oh…*" Chloe repeats.

"It's understandable. I have a past of worrying too much." Scratching the back of my head, I try to find the words to explain.

"You told Noah I was a killer?" Chloe's eyes

widen. "Does he still think that about me?"

"He never thought you were a killer."

"Well, that's good to hear," Chloe mutters, forehead creased. "You see a therapist?"

"I used to." Exhaling, I look through my windshield toward the bar.

"About two years ago, I called the police on a neighbor who I thought was kidnapped."

"Oh… shit." Chloe mutters, gasping.

"That's when I started seeing a therapist." I sit up straighter. "There was a woman who lived two houses down the street from yours. She looked just like a woman who I saw reported missing in the news at the time. Her name was Jenna; the missing woman." I shake my head. "But I was wrong. The woman who lived down the street from us, barely came out of her house. And when she did, it was only with her husband. And she always wore hats. Like she was hiding her face…"

Letting my words linger, I think about it and really, I never had a real plausible reason to think that woman was in danger, at all. I only had a weird feeling about her. Just like I did about Chloe.

I wasn't watching the couples house every day for months, like I did with Chloe though. I waited only two weeks before I made the conclusion that the woman was in danger and then I anonymously called the police.

Thinking about it now, I cringe. I was impulsive and I couldn't control my actions, just like when I marched over to Chloe's house and deemed her a serial killer to her face.

I understand why Noah worries about me.

"But it wasn't Jenna?" Chloe asks.

"Nope," I sigh. "The couple moved out three months after I ruined their dinner with police pounding on their door because of my exaggerated imagination. I watched the whole thing unfold from my window. The police went to their house about twenty minutes after I made the call."

I shift uncomfortably in my seat, still looking ahead at the bar. Theresa should be walking out any minute now.

"What happened after that? How do you know she wasn't abducted? That's kind of weird the couple moved out right after that happened. You said they just moved in at the time, right?"

"I know." I nod. "I watched the cops talk to them for a while before they left, and the couple went back inside their house. I called the police station and asked what happened that night, but the person who answered the phone only told me two officers checked out the situation and said the woman was safe. She was living there alone with her husband. I didn't believe them, so I knocked on the door and asked her myself the next day. She basically threatened to call the cops and got super defensive since she realized I was the person who called on them. Just as defensive as I would if somebody accused my husband of abducting me." I raise my eyebrows and look at Chloe.

Chloe nods in acknowledgement.

"When she threatened to call the police on me, I literally ran back home, avoided both of them every time I was outside, and then three months later, I saw them moving out."

"I don't know if I was the reason for their move or if that was just a coincidence. Anyway, that's not the first time I've exaggerated anything. That was just the most…dramatic time, I guess you can call it. That was the only time police were involved."

"Noah had me see a therapist right after that whole thing happened because Laura had only passed away two months before. He thought her death had something to do with my new form of anxiety. And it turned out, he was right. My therapist told me I believed our neighbor was in some sort of danger because I allowed my brain to believe it. Basically, it was a trauma response to losing Laura. Her death was out of my control. Therefore, I developed a lot of anxiety which causes me to imagine situations that aren't actually happening."

"Like you wanted that woman to be Jenna so you could save her because you couldn't save Laura?" Chloe summarizes.

"Actually… yeah," I huff a laugh. *I didn't think of it that way.* "My therapist didn't explain it that easily though."

Chloe shrugs, smiling. "I've had my share of therapy. Ellie, I killed my ex-boyfriend who I actually loved at the time. I was afraid of him, but still a part of me loved him. I know. It sounds ridiculous but I was heartbroken that day… but then I was happy, relieved, mostly. I have trauma too. Even though I don't regret what I did to my ex, I still talk to a therapist about what happened with him."

It turns out Chloe and I are more alike in different ways than I thought.

"I know you only became friends with me because you thought I was a killer, but I feel kind of glad we're here… well, not happy you thought I was a serial killer, but if Theresa is really responsible for the men who are missing in this town, then I hope we can at least help their families."

Chloe's right. At least she doesn't hate me and she's helping in my investigation.

"I'm sorry that I did that," I answer truthfully. I *am* sorry that I befriended her in the way I did but I am not sorry that we are sitting here either.

"You know, you're pretty brave to befriend me, then stay in my house all while thinking I'm capable of murder."

"Well, you *are*…" I shrug and Chloe bursts out into a loud laugh.

To be fair, I *was* right about Chloe. She's not a serial killer but she did kill a man.

26

We watched Theresa leave the Ghost bar and walk to her black SUV in the parking lot of the bar. From there, we followed her in my truck to another club a block over from the Ghost bar. When she pulled up in front of the entrance, the customer who we saw her kiss on the cheek earlier got in the passenger side.

After picking him up, she drove about twenty minutes to a neighborhood that is way more secluded than where Chloe and I live.

"If she lives here, she must be living with other people. Roommates or family." Chloe commented as we watched Theresa park her SUV in the driveway of a one-story home.

And Chloe was right. This house does not

look like it belongs to a single woman in her early twenties. White paint decorates the exterior of the house. Two large windows are on each side of a burgundy-colored front door. No garage but I see a large front yard and a fenced-in backyard. And just like Chloe's backyard; Theresa's leads right out to the woods, except hers is fenced-in.

The nearest houses in the neighborhood are about five hundred feet away from each other.

I parked my truck off the shoulder of the road in a patch of grass about three hundred feet from Theresa's.

Both Theresa and the guy from the bar stepped out of her SUV and walked right through the front door almost an hour ago. The sun is already up and I'm not home. Noah is due to text me any minute now.

"Can you see the number of the house?" I ask Chloe while grabbing my phone from the cupholder to search the property address.

"2367," Chloe answers leaning up to look through the windshield.

"And we're on Coolidge Street, right?" I mumble as I search for the address on my phone. I want to see who is listed as the resident here.

"Yeah, why?" Chloe asks.

"It says the property owner is some lady named Lana Garcia. And the residence name is Tiffany Burnes."

"Who's Tiffany?" Chloe scrunches her forehead.

I am about to ask the same thing but my attention gets diverted from my phone when I hear Chloe gasp. I look up to see the front door of the house opening.

There hadn't been any movement, no lights turning on, curtains opening on the windows, or any sign that anyone was in there until right now.

Theresa is heading toward her SUV.

And she's alone.

"Shit, I hope she doesn't come this way," Chloe whispers as if Theresa can hear us through the windows of my truck while we are parked nearly three hundred feet away.

But Theresa doesn't even look our way when she gets in the driver side of her vehicle. Seconds later, we see the brake lights shine and the reverse lights glow as she backs out of her driveway.

If she's looking this way and paying attention, she would notice my truck on the side of the road. I am hoping she will think it's just abandoned. That happens often in this town. I see broken down and unoccupied vehicles that are parked on the side of the road by the woods sometimes.

I don't realize I'm holding my breath until her SUV backs out onto the road and turns the opposite way of where we are parked.

"Holy shit," Chloe exhales, relief setting over her expression as she sinks down into her seat.

I wait until the vehicle is out of our sight before opening my door.

"What are we doing?" Chloe closes the passenger door of my truck and rushes to catch up to my pace.

"We're going to knock," I say as we approach the front door of the home and I pound both my fists on the dark wood. "Hello?"

No answer.

"Hello?" Chloe yells, knocking a little louder than me. She rings the doorbell.

No answer.

But I think I heard something.

It sounds like people talking. Their voices are not clear enough to make out what they're saying though.

"Do you hear that?" I whisper to Chloe.

She presses her ear against the door, nodding.

"Let's go look in the backyard. We need to find a gate. There's got to be a backdoor to this place, right?" I round the corner of the front yard on the right side of the house where a tall wooden fence begins.

There is no gate on this side of the fence though. No latch anywhere on the wood either. I walk a couple steps to see the perimeter of the fence.

No side gate or latch either.

"Maybe there's a gate on the other side." I run back to the front yard and around the left of the house. I hear Chloe following behind me.

No gate or latch over here either.

Instead of going back to the front yard, I continue walking along the perimeter of the fence toward the woods.

"Where are you going? Wait, I have an idea!" I hear Chloe shuffling behind me when I turn the corner of where the fence meets the tree line. There's just enough space for a person to walk between the woods and the fence.

And there's a gate right in the middle of the fence with a lock that needs a key on it.

"What the hell?" Chloe gasps when she catches up to me. "Who the hell puts a gate back here, directly to the forest? There's no point..."

"A serial killer," I mutter as I try to pull on the lock.

We need the key. Or some bolt cutters to get it open.

"Hold on." Chloe brings her key ring out from the front of her black sweatpants pocket. Then she pulls out something that does not look like a key off the ring.

It looks like a lock, like the one on the gate that we are trying to get open...

"I was just about to suggest we do this on the front door, but this might be easier for me," she says as she begins pulling out pin keys.

"What the hell?" I gesture to the lock in her hand.

"Lockpick set," Chloe answers. "My ex that I rented the house out with this year, used to change the locks when we would get into fights. He wasn't abusive toward me like Jarod was. But he was vindictive. I got savvy with lockpicking because of him. Told you, I haven't picked the best of men."

"That's for sure," I mumble.

But then I think about the first few months that Chloe moved in. *Why didn't I ever see that guy in the short amount of time he lived with her?* "I never noticed your ex living with you. What was his name?"

"Terrance," Chloe answers while continuing to do whatever it is she's doing to get the lock on the gate open.

Terrance. I found him online when I searched for Chloe. I know that I never saw him across the street from me. Even if he was only living with Chloe for two weeks. I would have remembered him…

"Did Terrance work?" I ask. "I never saw him. I didn't even see him help you move in. I only saw the movers."

Chloe stops lockpicking to look at me. She drops her shoulders, sighing. "He didn't work. He drank all day at home and barely left the house. If he left, it was probably in the middle of the night to go get more beer. You've really been watching me for a while, huh?" She shakes her head, huffing a disbelieving laugh.

I shrug and she continues lockpicking.

To think that I was suspicious of this woman being a threat, being a serial killer. As I continue to get to know Chloe even more, I am beginning to feel sorry for her. I feel sorry for the trauma and pain she's been through.

No wonder she sounded so weary of my husband when I first met her. Men have traumatized her. That's her first thought; not to trust them.

I can't imagine being locked out of your own house by your significant other.

I watch Chloe insert the different size tools into the gate lock and wiggle them until one properly fits.

Doubt is setting in that Chloe won't get this thing unlocked until a couple minutes later, I watch her yank open the lock and start to push the gate in.

27

October 8th
Thursday

Chloe's eyes enlarge as she gets first sight of the backyard. Once she pushes the gate open wider, I see the same view and immediately, I understand why she's holding such an expression on her face.

We are both staring at a normal looking backyard.

But it looks abnormally… normal.

Two green outdoor chairs and a white table are placed on the white painted deck outside of a white back door on the house.

And the grass is beautifully bright green. It's too green. Like its brand new; fake looking.

I walk on to the yard and kneel to tug at the greenery. The slick green texture lifts from the ground underneath my fingertips, but I don't pull it up completely.

"Artificial grass." I look up at Chloe.

The oddly pristine blue furniture and white exterior of the house, along with the fake grass is so normal that it's abnormal.

There is a small window above the handle on the backdoor of the house, so I walk up to press my forehead against the glass.

Chloe attempts to look through the large window on the right side of the door. "I can't see anything. The curtains are drawn. But I think I hear something again," she says.

Not only do I hear it, but I also see it.

We are hearing a TV that is mounted on the wall in the living room which is right in front of the window that Chloe is trying to look through. She can't see inside because black drapes are strung over the window. The only light inside of the living room is cascading from the TV.

An action movie is playing that I don't know the name of but there is a lot of noise from a fight scene on the screen. Guns are drawn; explosions are going off.

Nobody is watching the movie though. There isn't any sign of anyone being in the living room recently either. No drinks or food on top of the wood coffee table in front of the white couch.

What is it with all the white?

"We're hearing the TV. There's some movie playing," I tell Chloe. "I don't see anybody inside though."

When I look to the left through the window, there is a kitchen. Although I can't see too much of the inside from out here.

"Hello? Hello? Anybody in there?" I shout while knocking loudly on the door.

But I only receive gunshots and explosions from the TV as a response.

When I fail at turning the doorknob, I glance over at Chloe, prompting her to pull out her lockpick set again.

It takes her a couple minutes longer than it took to unlock the gate before she gets the back door open.

Slowly, we both step inside of the house.

"Hello?" I yell.

"Anyone here?" Chloe calls out.

Nothing but the sound of gunshots and explosions.

I walk over to the table where the remote is so I can mute the sound of the TV.

"Hello?" I yell again.

Eerie silence resonates through the house now that the TV is muted.

Chloe looks around the living room. "I wouldn't think Theresa's house would look like this."

"Me neither." I agree. It doesn't look like she has a roommate.

The living room is spotless, but the kitchen looks lived in. A small white table and two chairs are arranged next to the refrigerator in the corner of the kitchen. There is a bottle of empty margarita mix, and a handful of empty vodka and rum bottles on the counter. Dirty dishes fill up the sink.

"Maybe this is the guy's house and not Theresa's?" I think aloud to Chloe who has disappeared into the hallway near the living room.

"I don't think so." I hear her respond as I

notice a small door out of the kitchen that is slightly open just enough to reveal a tiny bathroom.

Hair products, makeup, and a few wigs lay around the sink counter and on the tile floor by the toilet. Then I see a black short wig that is lying on top of a pile of clothes.

"Ellie!" Chloe's voice alerts me.

I rush out of the bathroom past the living room and in the hallway.

I find three doors that are partly open and Chloe looking right up at the ceiling.

Right above her is an attic door with a lock on it; similar to the one that Chloe lockpicked on the fence.

"Do you smell that?" She looks at me warily.

Nodding, I scrunch my nose as I get closer.

I do smell that.

It's a smell I've never been around before but it's safe to say the expression *"smells like death"* suffices.

28

"Did you check those rooms?" I gesture toward the three doors in the hallway.

"No one's in any of them," She shakes her head, then looks back up at the attic. "I can get that unlocked. I need a chair."

"I saw one in the kitchen."

As Chloe heads to get a chair, I push open the first door on the left side in the hallway. It reveals another bathroom. This one is bigger, cleaner and not nearly as messy as the one in the front of the house near the kitchen. No wigs, clothes, or makeup laying around. Just two red towels hanging on the wall, hand soap and one toothbrush on the sink counter.

I push open the next door in the hallway. This looks like a spare bedroom. All that is in here is a bed without any sheets, no pillows or a blanket, and a white dresser. The closet is empty. I turn around to look in the last room across the hallway.

This room is clearly Theresa's bedroom. Mixed in a pile of dirty clothes, I immediately spot several pairs of the Ghost Go-Go cocktail waitresses shorts on the floor. Then I see red colored cocktail dresses with the name *Club Fate* on them hanging in her closet.

I have not had the opportunity to confirm whether Theresa works at Club Fate or whether Chloe lied to me until now.

Chloe's words still stand true.

Bright colored tank tops, several pairs of jean shorts, and a few dresses take up the hangers in Theresa's closet. Along with perfume bottles and jewelry, tons of makeup containers cover the top of her dresser. The bed is also a complete mess.

I step back out into the hallway when Chloe pulls up the chair she found in the kitchen. She places the chair directly under the attic door and steps on top of it to reach the lock.

After a few minutes, she smiles down at me once the lock opens, and she begins to pull the ladder staircase down to the floor.

"Holy shit," she gasps, covering her mouth as she starts to ascend the stairs. "The smell…"

It's potent.

I climb up the ladder behind Chloe once I have enough room, until her foot nearly kicks me in the face as she gets to the top of the attic.

She stopped climbing. Her body is still. Her eyes are locked on whatever it is she sees in the attic.

Silently, she moves slightly out of the way to

give me enough room to climb past her and see what she's in awe of.

Tied by rope around his wrists and legs; the man who we saw get out of her SUV, is lying unconscious on top of plastic sheeting on the floor in the right corner of the attic.

29

"Holy shit!" Chloe gasps while holding onto the top of the steps. "We need to help him!"

On the left side of the attic, an axe, a chainsaw, several containers of bleach, and a toolbox are placed on top of another large piece of plastic wrap.

Six more rolls of plastic wrap, sized as large as six feet, are rolled up against the wall.

"Holy shit, holy shit," Chloe keeps muttering as we approach the man on the floor.

Slowly bending down, I nudge his bicep softly, trying not to alarm him.

Chloe kneels next to me. I nudge his arm again. This time, harder.

When I do, his eyes slowly open only for a

moment before he quickly moves back away from us in fear. But dizziness takes over and he falls back down.

"We're here to help!" Chloe stammers, struggling to reassure him. "We're going to untie you! We're going to get you out of here!"

This poor guy looks terrified.

And really fucked up. Not just drunk. Theresa must have drugged him with something.

We need to cut the rope to get him out of here before she comes back because it sure as hell looks like she plans to.

I look over to the other side of the attic where the axe and toolbox are. There is a large cutting knife in the mix of tools, so I crawl over the plastic sheeting to grab it.

Once the knife is in my hand, I spot the dried blood stains on it.

We need to all get out of here now. I did not think of any crazy delusional theory. My theory was never a theory. This is real. And I need to finally go to the police about it. *Noah is going to be pissed.*

After several tries of cutting the rope loose around the man's feet and hands, it loosens and releases him freely.

He attempts to stand up, but I assume that whatever Theresa drugged him with has taken over his system because he falls on his knees.

He can hardly keep his body up straight.

"H--how did you find me?" He looks toward the ladder, slurring his words. "Wh-where is the bitch?"

"We need to get you out of here!" As I sling his left arm around my shoulder, I spot a large gash just above his neck. The back of his head is dripping blood.

Theresa must have knocked him over the head with something. So, maybe he isn't drugged. He might be just falling out of consciousness because his head keeps bleeding out.

"He's bleeding. We need to get him to a hospital! I think that's why he keeps passing out!" I tell Chloe as she tries to put his right arm around her neck to help me hold him up straight. "Oh my God," she grunts because this man is dead weight heavy and has just fallen unconscious again.

Chloe picks his head up, then to both my surprise and his, she slaps the right side of his face, awakening him.

"We need you to crawl!" Chloe starts dragging him across the floor, I jump in to help; all three of us fumbling to get to the ladder.

Finally, we're able to sit him down with his legs dangling on the top of the first few steps.

Chloe climbs the stairs first so she can help assist him down the steps. I remain in the attic to hold him up by his arms.

But as soon as we try to carry him down, we both immediately fail. We are literally no help to this man.

He's awake enough to try to hold on to the steps of the ladder for only a few seconds before he ends up sliding down the steps and landing on top of Chloe on the floor in the hallway.

But it looks like the fall must have jolted him awake because now he's struggling to roll off her and is getting up to his knees.

Quickly, I climb down as Chloe is already

limping to stand up on her feet.

"What's your name?" I ask him.

"J--Jake," he stammers. His eyes keep fluttering in and out of consciousness.

"We're taking you to the hospital." I try to reassure him but all I can hear is my heart pounding.

30

We tried to take Jake to the hospital instead of waiting in my truck for the police and paramedics, but he refused. Through falling in and out of unconsciousness, Jake said he wanted to remain outside in case she came back home.

But Theresa never did. At least, she didn't show up in the time that we remained outside her house.

We managed to keep Jake awake by holding Chloe's hoodie over the gash on the back of his head.

I don't think it stopped the bleeding completely. I just hope we at least helped him.

Once the two police officers and paramedics arrived, Jake got checked out and tried to tell the police what happened to him. Although, he couldn't remain awake long enough to tell them everything. Besides saying his name and address, he reassured the police that Chloe and I saved him from the attic, and he met Theresa at the Ghost bar. She picked him up from another bar later on in the night (which both Chloe and I saw, and confirmed) then she took him to her house where she made them drinks.

And that was the last of what Jake could explain before the paramedics took him to the hospital.

Which is when the questioning against me and Chloe began.

Our statement: We had a suspicion that Theresa had something to do with Malik's disappearance because Chloe saw Theresa leave the bar with Malik around the time he went missing (which is true).

So therefore, we decided to watch Theresa right after we noticed that coincidence. We followed her home from the bar this morning, saw her go into the house with Jake, then we heard a noise in the house and ran in to help. (Sort of true. I mean, we did hear the TV and we did believe Jake was in danger.)

"How did you get inside of the house? Did you know Theresa wasn't there?" The first police officer that arrived on scene had asked us.

And our response: "Theresa left her front door unlocked. We heard the noise from my truck, so we got out and knocked on her door. We knocked a few times, but no one answered. Then we tried the doorknob. It opened so we walked in."

Admitting to the police that Chloe broke into the house by lockpicking the gate, the backdoor and also the attic, would not be beneficial to our story.

But I did explain a part of the truth as well. I told the police officer that I had an interest in missing people in town, and I linked a few disappearances to Theresa being responsible.

Then I thoughtlessly brought out my evidence board to further prove what I figured out.

I say *thoughtlessly* because after willingly handing my board over to the police, I am not sure what happened since I have been sitting in the police station with Chloe for half an hour now.

The officer who took our statement in front of Theresa's house instructed us to follow him back here while several other officers stayed at the scene.

Noah has been texting and calling me repeatedly until I just turned my phone off a few minutes ago. It is way too late in the morning for me not to be home. I have no excuse. I will need to tell him the truth after I get out of here today.

That's if I get out of here today...

Just when I am starting to think that we should be looking for a lawyer, and maybe it is time I tell my husband what's going on, one of the detectives who introduced herself when we first arrived at the station, finally walks in the room. I think she called herself Detective Carner.

The Detective lets out an exhale before she pulls up a chair in front of us. She takes a seat, not directly like an interrogation (I believe we've already sort of gone through that in front of Theresa's house) but she angles the chair diagonally toward us. Like she's our friend about to do business.

We're not in an interrogation room though. Instead, we are sitting in a glass cubicle in the police station's lobby. I can see the entrance and exit from here.

But this feels weird. It doesn't feel right. Maybe I should turn my phone back on and call Noah now.

And also a lawyer.

31

October 8 th

Thursday

"Ladies, how are you both doing?" Detective Carner asks.

I look at Chloe who shares my same exasperated expression. We swap looks quietly.

The Detective accepts our silence as an answer.

"I understand it's been a tough couple of hours," she smiles. "I just got back from speaking to Jake in the hospital. He is conscious and has given me his statement already."

"Oh, so he's okay!" Chloe sits up in her chair, relief settling over her. "Oh, thank God!"

"Yes. He was able to tell me what happened."

"Oh! That's so good to hear!" I let out a relieved breath.

"So, let me get this straight," Detective Carner loses the smile. "You two told one of the officers on the scene, that you had a *hunch* that Theresa was suspected in Malik Jensen's disappearance because you—," Detective Carner directs her attention to Chloe who is starting to sink back in her chair. "Chloe, you saw Theresa leave the bar with Malik around the time he went missing?"

Chloe's chest is heaving in and out. Her breath slows for a moment, followed by a long exhale. Her body stiffens. She's nervous. We rehearsed her explanation while we were waiting for the police and paramedics with Jake in my truck.

"Yes. When Ellie showed me Malik's photo on her evidence board, I immediately thought of Theresa. I remember seeing Theresa with Malik just a few weeks ago at work. I don't know if I saw him on the same night that he got reported missing though," she swallows.

"Ellie said she thought her suspect worked two places. The same bar I work at, the Ghost Go-Go bar and possibly Club Fate. Then I realized Theresa had mentioned to me once before that she works at Club Fate a few times a week when she's not working at the Ghost bar. I've hung out with Theresa only a few times outside of the bar but we're not really friends…I've never been to Club Fate, but anyways, I saw Ellie's notes and well, this is all sort, of… it's kind of coincidental."

This is the statement we both agreed on in my truck. Except Chloe's delivery did not sound as strong as she practiced it before coming here.

If we tell this detective the entire truth, she won't take us seriously.

If I admit to originally thinking Chloe was a murderer and obsessively watching her for months, how I figured out a pattern in Avery's missing persons by simply analyzing their online database, and then I confronted Chloe out of impulsive rage thinking she was the killer; honestly, I would end up making myself look delusional.

Even though I'm not delusional in the slightest.

This Detective would not take us seriously at all. None of what I did would make our story sound credible even though it's the truth.

This whole situation seems… unreal.

But it's happening.

Unlike the time I thought my neighbor was being held captive and she wasn't. I was wrong then and I have acknowledged that. Just like I admit that I was wrong about Chloe.

But I was not wrong about a female serial killer in this town.

So, just like I have been lying to my husband, we're fibbing our truth to the police so that our truth is believable because we know how the truth really sounds; *unbelievable.*

The truth would divert the police away from what's really important. The fact that we caught a serial killer who the police were never searching for or had any idea about.

At least, not that I know of. I don't think Avery Police knew about Theresa before we just brought it to their attention.

"Ellie, what made you look into Malik's disappearance in the first place? What made you start your investigation board?" Detective Carner moves her gaze at me.

I prepared a response too. My turn now.

"I got an Amber Alert regarding a teenage girl a few months ago. Her name was Bianca." I clear my throat. "And it made me wonder how many other people are missing in this town. Avery isn't super small but still, it's a small enough town, you know?" I stop to see Detective Carner's reaction.

It's blank, so I keep talking.

"Well, like I said, I got curious and decided to look at everyone else on the missing persons database. That's when I noticed that Steven, Theo, Devon and Ryan all went missing almost a month apart from each other. Then Malik popped up as the next disappearance a few months later."

I look briefly at Chloe before I keep going. She's looking down at her feet.

Not helpful.

I continue. "I had shown Chloe the database before Malik showed up on the list because I was telling her about how I was interested in the missing men, so when I showed her Malik's picture, she recognized him and said she saw him with Theresa at their job. So… I kind of went to see Theresa's interactions with her customers at the Ghost bar over the past few weeks, and I noticed that she was flirting with Jake more than the rest of her customers last night. I suggested to Chloe that we follow Theresa after their shift ends to see where she goes because it looked like Theresa was going to meet up with Jake later on… and well, she did."

My explanation sounded better when I rehearsed it with Chloe in the truck.

Chloe's expression is not giving me any

comfort either.

The detective nods while looking at both of us, eyebrows raised. "Why did it look like Theresa and Jake were going to meet after work?"

"Well, because we saw them exchange numbers when she was serving him at the Ghost bar and so, I just assumed." I shrug.

I'm being honest here.

Detective Carner is slowly nodding her head. "Ellie, were you at the Ghost bar last night only to watch Theresa? Did you plan to watch her before arriving there?"

"N--no," I stutter. "I sometimes hang out at the bar when Chloe's working there on nights I can't sleep." I shift in my seat. "I couldn't sleep last night. I have insomnia."

Again, Chloe's expression doesn't give me any reassurance. After all the information I have learned about liars and how many times I have deceived my husband over the past couple of months, you would think I would have handled this situation better.

But lying to a detective is another sense of bravery that I have not learned to achieve yet.

"So, you both followed Theresa and Jake from the bar that you work at," Detective Carner directs her eyes at Chloe, then back to me. "Then you both trespassed into Theresa's home because you heard a noise while you were sitting outside of her house in your truck, Ellie?"

I nod. "Yes."

"How long after following her home from the bar, did you hear a noise? And what was the noise you heard?"

"About an hour," I admit.

"We heard an argument," Chloe adds, sitting back up in her chair.

Well, we did. We heard the argument on the TV along with the gunshots and explosions.

Detective Carner is looking at us with a muddled expression.

I am starting to realize we didn't think all our responses through.

I turned on my phone right before Detective Carner walked in, but I didn't get a chance to call or text Noah back yet.

I wish I called a lawyer on the way here too.

I am also starting to wish I handled this whole thing differently from the beginning.

But then again, nobody would have taken me seriously if I didn't wait this long to get my facts straight.

"Was last night the only time you both followed Theresa home or anywhere around town?" Detective Carner asks the both of us. However, she only stares at me when she speaks.

"Yes," Chloe and I mumble together.

"Do you both know that you not only committed a crime, a couple crimes, but you also put yourselves in incredible danger?"

Chloe and I remain silent, exchanging wide-eyed expressions.

But Detective Carner goes on before we can say anything. "In spite of putting yourselves in danger, because of your brave acts, you two saved Jake from dying of an overdose. Theresa drugged him with various narcotics that she mixed into alcoholic drinks once they got back to her house."

I saw the empty margarita mix and liquor bottles on the kitchen counter…

"According to Jake, Theresa said she wanted to show him her music studio up there. All he can remember is climbing up the ladder, smelling something horrible. Then once he got upstairs it was dark and he went to ask where the light was, then felt something hit the back of his head. The next thing Jake could recall was waking up and seeing you two in front of him."

"Holy shit," Chloe whispers, shaking her head.

So the empty liquor bottles and margarita mix I saw on her counter once had substances that caused Jake to be unconscious.

But where was the object she used to knock him out? What did she use to cause the back of his head to bleed? I remember seeing an Axe on the table in the attic, but it didn't have blood on it. I don't recall seeing anything else up there that would have been heavy enough to use.

"What did she hit him over the head with?" I ask, sitting up straighter.

"We aren't sure yet," Detective Carner responds.

Chloe slouches back in her seat. Her breath is becoming steadier. I can only imagine what she is feeling. She's been through a version of this before, getting questioned by the police. And it doesn't look like she's handling it so well right now.

"So now what happens?" I ask. "Did you arrest Theresa yet?"

"Are we going to jail for trespassing?" Chloe adds, her eyes moving from me to the detective nervously.

"Or stalking?" I murmur.

Chloe's eyes protrude when she hears me.

"Neither." Detective Carner slightly smiles. This time, it looks genuine. "Thanks to the connections in the disappearances, you displayed on your board, Ellie, you have provided enough circumstantial evidence to begin an investigation into Theresa. We have a warrant to search her house and property and an investigative team is in the works now. We also have an APB out for Theresa and Avery Police are blocking off a perimeter around her neighborhood."

"Why didn't she come back for Jake?" I think out loud.

Clearly, Theresa planned to finish what she started, but why did she leave Jake alone up there, unconscious and tied up? It didn't look like she was in a hurry when we watched her leave the house without him before we broke in.

"I haven't figured that out yet," The detective answers honestly.

"Ellie!"

Just when I am about to ask Detective Carner if Chloe and I can leave, Noah's voice echoes through the thick glass cubicle from across the lobby.

"Noah?" I look toward the door. *Shit.*

I can see him looking at me through the window of the room we're in. Two police officers are stopping him from walking toward us, keeping him near the entrance of the station.

"That's my husband," I say to the detective.

"Stay here." Detective Carner leaves the room and I watch her walk up to Noah in the lobby.

"He looks angry," Chloe mutters,

"He probably thought I was dead or kidnapped," I sigh, slightly mortified that my husband is barreling in the station looking for me like I'm a child.

But I know he doesn't mean it like that. He loves me. He's worried. I get it.

Through the glass, I see Detective Carner say something to him as she points toward us, then she leads him back into the room we're in.

His horrified pale expression is slowly coming back to life once he approaches me. "What's going on?"

"I'm okay. Sorry to worry you, babe. How did you know I was here?" I get up quickly to hug him.

"I didn't!" He releases from our hug. "I came here to report you missing! I didn't expect to find you here. I went to Chloe's house. Nobody answered the damn door. Her Jeep wasn't in the driveway. I went to the bar where you said you were at last night and I didn't see your truck. I have no idea who the hell Theresa is, so I was going to just report you missing! That's why I walked in here just now. What the hell, Ellie?"

I forgot I sent a text to Noah, telling him that I was going to hang out at a friend's house. And I told him her name was Theresa.

Yes, I deceived him once again. I said another lie, but if you want to get technical, I also told the truth.

I *was* at Theresa's. Just not hanging out with her and sobering up.

And she's also obviously not my friend.

"I'm really, really sorry. It's a long story," I

say to Noah, then I turn to face Detective Carner. "Detective, are we in trouble? Can Chloe and I go home now?"

Noah looks over at the Detective, then at Chloe who is still sitting slumped down in her seat.

As she looks up at him, she looks confused, probably a bit frightened because of his body language and angry expression.

But like I told her, Noah is upset because he thought I was in danger. I know he's mad because he thought I was hurt or like I said dead, when I was sitting right here safe and sound in a police station, ignoring his calls and text messages.

"You two are not in trouble," Detective Carner responds.

"Oh, thank you!" Chloe stands up.

"But I am sending a police escort to follow you both home and sit outside your houses for the time being until I get more information on Theresa."

"Why?" Chloe gasps. "It's not like she knows that we were at her house… Does she?"

"We don't know what Theresa knows," Detective Carner says. "I am certain that she was going to come back for Jake and finish what she intended to do but you two stopped her. If Theresa drove back into the neighborhood while you two were waiting outside the house, or when my team first got there, we might not have noticed her in the area because we didn't know to look for her yet. We can't be too sure of anything, but I want to be cautious for your safety, that's all."

"Great." Chloe sits back down in her chair, exhaling. Tears are building up in her eyes. Just like her, I was hoping this would be over tonight.

But it seems like it's just the beginning.

"Please, ladies. Try not to be alarmed. You will be safe with a police car sitting outside between your houses for the next few days. I will have two patrol cars switch shifts throughout the day. You told one of my officers earlier that you live across the street from each other, right?"

Chloe and I nod. Within every word Detective Carner says, Noah's confused expression increases. From the detective, Chloe, and to me, his head is on a constant swivel.

"Ellie, before I let you go home though—" Detective Carner starts walking toward the door. "I need you to come explain your notes off that evidence board of yours. I need to hear your perspective."

As I am about to respond, suddenly my husband starts to chuckle.

Chloe, Detective Carner, and I exchange strange looks at Noah.

"Now I get why you're here," Noah says to me, shaking his head.

"Actually, no. You don't get it at all," I smirk.

3 2

"My name is Detective Carner, Chief Detective of Avery Police, and I am here today to announce that I have issued an arrest warrant out for Tiffany Burnes who goes by the name of Theresa. We do not know where she currently is, but we do know she is considered dangerous, especially to men who are in their twenties and early thirties. Theresa, again, also goes by the alias of Tiffany, is responsible for the death of eight men. Five of those men have been identified and their families have all been notified by now. According to the coroner reports from the autopsies done on the victims, the three unidentified victims were sadly murdered within the past two years and were between their mid-twenties to early thirties at the time of their passing. Theresa, again also with a confirmed Alias as Tiffany, is known to change her appearance through several styled wigs and wardrobe. The photo that I am sharing today is the most recent and accurate photo that we have of her. Avery Police station is offering a five-thousand-dollar reward for information leading to her arrest."

Good job Detective Carner. And you're welcome for utilizing the photo that I snuck of Theresa at the Go-Go bar before I brought her to your attention.

With a national televised announcement like what I just watched, along with Theresa's photo plastered on the screen, everyone that pays attention to the news or the internet in general, should know who Theresa is.

Wherever the hell she is; And whoever the hell she is.

Tiffany Burnes is supposedly Theresa's real name. However, when I search for Tiffany Burnes online, I do not find anything that matches the Theresa that I met.

That isn't stopping me from looking for her though.

Thanks to me; Steven, Devon, Ryan, Theo, and Malik were the five out of eight victims that have been identified and found in Theresa's backyard beneath the artificial grass that I once tried to lift.

The coroner's reports are starting to come back in. So far, they conclude that most of the men passed away from either a head trauma or a narcotic overdose. Or a combination of both.

That leads Avery police to believe that likely what Theresa did to Jake; how she drugged and assaulted him in the attic, she probably did with the rest of her victims.

The police and I speculate that Theresa drugged the men through margaritas. Then she probably used the same music studio lie that she used to lure Jake up to the attic to the rest of her victims.

She likely lured each man up there, already drunken and incoherent, then hit them over the head as soon as they climbed upstairs. By the time they went up in the attic, they were probably too fucked up from the drugs and they didn't have the cognition to climb back down the ladder or fight her when she hit them over the back of the head.

Through the autopsy reports, imprints on the flesh of each man's skull, revealed a two-inch-wide heart shaped tool that was used as Theresa's choice of weapon to knock the men unconscious.

Police have swept Theresa's house for anything heart shaped in that size multiple times but haven't found anything yet. That leads me to believe there is a good chance she still has the weapon with her, or she got rid of it.

And whatever that weapon is, I have yet to figure it out.

But I plan to.

Since fragments of the deceased male remains were scattered throughout her backyard, it is clear that the Axe I saw in the attic was utilized to make that happen. Detective Carner will not confirm that theory directly with me, but I know it is true.

The Axe was only clean when Chloe and I showed up because we halted her plan before she could complete it. I am sure that Axe had been filled with blood many times before we saw it.

According to the timeframe of when the three unidentified men passed away, I believe they might have been Theresa's first victims. Maybe none of the men were ever reported missing.

Or maybe, they were not residents in the town of Avery. They could have been reported missing to another police station in another town or city. Maybe Theresa met the other men outside of Avery and drove back to her house with them.

All I can do is speculate on the numerous possibilities.

Detective Carner is still looking into missing persons within the surrounding towns and cities police departments.

She explained to me that if a person isn't in the system as missing, or if they do not have a criminal background, arrest history, or prior convictions, it will be harder to find out each of their identities. The bodies are so decomposed; the coroners only have the bones to work with.

I know all of this because Detective Carner gave me this information after I called her several times over the past month.

I just dialed her number for the first time today. At the same time, a knock on my front door alerts me that Chloe is here. I told her to walk over so she can hear our conversation.

"Hi, Detective. It's Ellie," I say into the phone as I open the door for Chloe.

"Yes, Hello. Ellie," Detective Carner answers except her tone of voice sounds like she regrets it.

I set my phone on speaker and rest it on top of

my living room table. I sit down next to Chloe on the sofa.

"Any new update?" I ask.

"No update yet, Ellie. I'm sorry."

"Did you talk to anybody in Theresa's family yet?" I lean onto my knees, closer to my phone.

"Yes. We did that already." The tone in the detective's voice sounds as if she is trying to tell me that's what her job entails so obviously, she looked into it.

Yeah, but she wasn't doing such a good job before I stepped in, so it's a valid question in my opinion.

"We spoke to Theresa's mother and older sister. They have not seen or had any contact with her," Detective Carner goes on. "So far, they have been cooperative with me, and I don't have any reason to believe either one of them knew what she was doing or where she currently is. However, they both live two hours South of Avery and I have a friend who works in their cities department. He has an officer do occasional drive-bys in their neighborhood, but so far, no sign of Theresa."

Yeah because that woman plans to set foot back in Avery. Theresa, Tiffany, whatever the fuck her name is, she's probably long out of this town by now.

"Police escort," Chloe whispers, nudging my arm.

Through the blinds of my front window, I see the same police car that's been parked on my street since midnight.

Two officers usually park their unmarked vehicles outside, switching watch duty mornings and nights since the day we saved Jake two weeks ago. Another unmarked police car supposedly has been following Chloe to work but she hasn't ever noticed anybody.

"Are you taking away the police escort anytime soon?" I ask Detective Carner.

"Unfortunately, I may have to remove the patrol cars in the next couple days, but I will prepare you before I make that decision."

Chloe mouths to me the word, *Gianna.*

At the police station, when explaining my evidence board, I told the detective about Gianna even though she never really seemed suspicious to me. It just seemed like she knew Theresa more than Chloe did, and as far as Chloe knew, she believed Gianna and Theresa were closer in friendship too.

But Chloe said Gianna seemed just as shocked as all of her other coworkers were when they first found out about Theresa a month ago.

"Detective, I haven't asked you about Gianna yet. Have you spoken to her?"

"Yes, Ellie. We interviewed her already. She was not very close with Theresa. Unfortunately, she couldn't give me any helpful information about her. Gianna said she only hung out with Theresa outside of work only a handful of times. She said Theresa usually invited her out and a couple of those times were with your friend, Chloe."

I look at Chloe whose forehead is scrunched. "Same with me," she whispers. "Theresa always invited us out…"

"Interesting," I mutter. "Are you sure that Gianna doesn't know anything about Theresa? Are you sure she wasn't lying?"

"Yes, Ellie. I am sure." Detective Carner clears her throat. "Gianna also had an alibi during the timeframe of most of the disappearances. She was either working at her other job, which is a 24/7 diner called Lester's or she was at home with her roommate. She wasn't even scheduled to work at the Ghost bar, and neither was she there during the nights when Ryan, Steven and Malik were there. We looked into it and spoke with the manager. Her alibi checks out."

"So now what?" I sigh, picking up the phone off my coffee table and leaning back against the sofa.

"It's only been two weeks, Ellie. I know that's two weeks too long, but I am confident we will find Theresa. We are interviewing all the right people, including everyone at both of her work places. I will find her. I want to assure you of that. You have been very helpful in this case, and I thank you for your efforts. I will call you if I need anything more from you. But until then, please know that I have this handled." Detective Carner sounds like she is ready to end the conversation, but I am not.

"Before we hang up," I say. "Detective, if you can't find Tiffany, how long will it take until you stop searching for her?"

"I'll never stop searching for her."
Neither will I.

January

3 3

"How have you been feeling?"

"Fine."

"Fine, how?"

"Just… fine?" I shrug.

I'd feel better than fine if I weren't sitting in this small bedroom made into an office right now.

"Okay. Let's start with why you're here."

"That's the thing, I only called you for an appointment because my husband told me I should see you."

"He cares about you."

"I know."

"He wants to make sure you're okay."

"Yes." I grit my teeth. "I know."

Silence resonates in the air of my therapist's, Stephanie's office which is on the first floor of her two-story home.

I have always found it strange for a therapist to work from their own house. Especially because they deal with mental health patients. Sure, not everybody that goes to therapy is dangerous. I certainly am not. Although, I am sure Stephanie sees a couple of patients who are.

I know the longer I hold out in explaining why I called to make an appointment after nearly two and a half years, the longer I will sit in this room. And I have already been in this chair for ten minutes; Ten minutes that have felt more like an hour.

So, I begin to tell her every detail. Every detail about what occurred within the past year of my life. From obsessively watching Chloe across the street and befriending her out of ulterior motives, to truly becoming real friends and how I impulsively accused Chloe of killing, which led me to figuring out who the real killer of Avery was.

I even tell Stephanie about how often I lied to my husband during that time, along with the crimes I committed. I snuck onto Chloe's property, and I broke into Theresa's house. (Although technically that was Chloe who did the breaking into Theresa's. I was just an accomplice).

I tell Stephanie that I moved my camera specifically to see Chloe's front door, knowing it wasn't morally right and probably illegal in some way. And how I looked for the victim's families online and reached out to each person online and in person. (Technically that wasn't really a crime, but I know that wasn't morally right either.)

When I am done talking, I notice by the clock on Stephanie's desk that nine minutes have passed.

I need to stop rambling.

Stephanie draws her head back. "Okay, then."

"It was a lot. I know," I sigh. Going over everything out loud is admittedly just a bit embarrassing.

But imagine if I had been wrong about a serial killer living here in our town though?

I think that would have been even more embarrassing; being wrong. Again.

"Well, Ellie. This situation is very different from when you first started seeing me," Stephanie says.

"I know. This time, I was right. This time, I'm not crazy." I cross my arms at my torso, shrugging.

"Nobody ever called you crazy besides yourself, Ellie."

"I wasn't acting very sane when you first met me, you have to admit." I roll my eyes. "And not as of lately either. Even though my insanity actually led me to catching a killer this time," I sigh. "Well, almost…"

"I saw on the news yesterday that Theresa or Tiffany, I heard she goes by both names; she hasn't been caught yet," Stephanie nods. "Had I known you were involved in identifying her, I would have called you for a session *before* you called me."

Stephanie's response causes a genuine laugh out of me. I forgot she can be funny sometimes. "Well, here I am now."

"Have you told Noah about all the times you lied to him?" she asks.

"He knows that I wasn't so truthful over the past few months," I shrug.

I have not directly told Noah how many times

I lied, but I am sure that he knows the night he found me in the police station was not the first time I hadn't been completely honest with him. Especially when he found out my board of evidence still existed after I promised him that it was gone.

"How are you and Noah doing now? Was he angry with you for lying?"

"We're fine. He was upset at first, not mad at me. He was just hurt. But he understood why I didn't tell him the truth. He knows that I would never intentionally keep anything from him in a malicious way. I was just worried he wouldn't take me seriously, which he really wasn't taking me seriously at the time. I showed him my board before. Not on purpose but still, he saw it and he didn't think I should take it to the police when I tried explaining everything. Noah never directly said he didn't believe me …" My words drag. "But I don't know…"

This is hard to explain because I admit that my actions over the past few months were impulsive. Thinking my own neighbor is a killer and there I was befriending her…

Noah is upset that I couldn't tell him the truth. Although at the same time, given my history with calling the police on a woman who wasn't in any danger with really no proof at all, he understands why I was conflicted.

"Are you still friends with Chloe?" Stephanie asks.

"Yes, still friends." I shift in my seat.

"Have you told her everything you told me? The things you did before you became true friends? Like when you were watching her through your window or when you walked over to her house while she wasn't home?"

"She knows about some things I've done," I answer.

"She still lives across from you?" Stephanie asks.

I nod.

"And you talk often?"

"Yeah, about once a week or so."

"Well, that's one good thing that happened to you over the past few months, despite everything, right? A new friend? You haven't had a friend since Laura passed away." Stephanie crosses her leg over the other. "Or have you? I'm sorry. I shouldn't assume. That's rude of me. It's been a little while since we talked, Ellie."

Fourteen minutes left of our session.

"No, you're right," I sigh. "Chloe is my first friend since Laura died."

"Even though you and Chloe became friends in a…" Stephanie scrunches her nose, "—in an unusual way, I think it's good for you to maintain your friendship with her."

Stephanie's right. Chloe and I are a lot closer than ever now. I wouldn't call her my new best friend, but we do hang out once a week. Sometimes, we eat takeout at her place while other times, we have coffee at mine. And we try our best to forget about Theresa.

It's hard though.

Stephanie nods, letting silence sit in the air, keeping her gaze on me.

I hate when she does that. She is expecting me to keep talking to break the awkward silence between us.

"And how are you feeling with Theresa still being on the run?"

"I…" Sitting back against the cushion on the couch, I exhale. "I just wish the police would catch her, but I don't think they're going to." My leg involuntarily shakes. The whole thing irritates me. "Three months. It's been three months already. I don't get it. They even identified all the bodies by now."

"Oh, I hadn't heard that," Stephanie says.

"Yeah," I nod. "The police confirmed the three men were all reported missing in different cities. Just like my original thought," I huff a laugh. "And still, nobody can find her. If it weren't for me, well for Chloe too, Tiffany/ Theresa, whatever the hell her name is, she wouldn't even be on the police radar. Nobody was even looking into those men's disappearances until I brought it to their attention."

"You sound irritated."

"It's irritating. I don't understand how the police can't find her. I don't even understand why they didn't spot a pattern in any of the disappearances, when I did." I exhale. "Literally, all I did was study the database, then questioned the right people. It was right in front of my face. It didn't take me too long to put together, so I don't understand why the police never noticed what I noticed. My focus was just on the wrong person at first."

Stephanie sits back in her chair. "Maybe it was because you were looking for something. You were looking for a pattern."

"Isn't that the police's job though? To look for a pattern? Especially if it involves missing people of their own town?" My eyes roll.

"Not unless they have a suspicion or a reason to look into anyone."

Well, shit. That's logical. I didn't think about it that way.

The police never began an investigation until I brought it to their attention because they never had a reason to connect any of the men's disappearances together.

Who would have thought those men were targeted by only one person?

No one.

My reason began with a thought of Chloe looking suspicious. How my suspicions led me to Theresa as the real killer is merely what you could call almost small-town irony.

"So, what are you up to in life now, Ellie? Still working at the collection job?"

I nod, smiling.

Stephanie tilts her head to the left which means she is about to ask me a question that I probably don't want to answer or talk about. "Ellie, I have to ask."

I look at her, innocently shrugging. "What's up?"

"Have you been investigating Theresa on your own? Have you started a new investigation on Theresa like you did when you were suspecting Chloe?"

Yes, I have. And this time, nobody is going to know about it until I find the woman myself.

"No." I shake my head.

"Do you plan to?"

"No. I'll leave it to the police. It's not my job." I smile while keeping eye contact with

Stephanie.

Good liars tend to keep good eye contact.

I have been practicing what I spent time in learning.

"And how have you been sleeping?"

Like absolute shit. The look on Jake's face when he woke up in the attic and saw us will always be engraved in my memory.

But I sure as hell will not tell Stephanie that.

"I had a rough first few nights but I'm good now. I've been sleeping through the night without any problems," I say, as I get ready to gather my purse.

Two more minutes left.

"Any dreams?"

I shake my head, no.

"Have you spoken to Jake after that night?"

I nod. "I spoke to him a few days later. He received both mine and Chloe's phone numbers from the Detective and called to tell us how grateful he was that we saved his life." I slightly grin. "He also swore that he is going to make Theresa go to prison when the police catch her. Even though they have plenty of evidence to charge her, he plans to testify and help in her arrest as much as he's needed. He's her only surviving victim." I stand up. "That the police know of."

"I'm very proud of you. Ellie."

"Thanks," I murmur.

Stephanie looks over at the clock on top of her desk. "Well, Ellie. That's it for today unless you have anything else you want to talk about with me?"

"Not really."

"Let's schedule another session next week,

Tuesday. Does 2:00 p.m. work for you?"

"That works," I agree as I head to walk out of the door of her office. "See you then."

When I walk through her house unsupervised, I get the urge to snoop around.

Really, why are doctors so trusting of their patients? If I was truly impulsive, I would act upon my urge but I'm not impulsive.

I am just a curious person which isn't always a bad thing.

Sometimes curiosity doesn't always kill the cat.

1 Year Later

3 4

As I am logging into my work portal, I hear the text notification sound from my phone.

It's from a number that I don't recognize.

Ding. Another new text; a long paragraph.

Ding. And again.

Ding. Another paragraph.

Several more dings, and more paragraphs appear on my screen.

One after another.

And another.

I scroll all the way to the top until eventually the messages stop coming in. I begin to read from the beginning.

ELLIE! You little curious bitch! You thought you would get me caught but you thought wrong!

THE WOMAN I BEFRIENDED

I knew you and Chloe were on to me when you started coming to the bar more often than usual last year. I saw the tension at first, how you both looked at me and kept whispering like little high school gossip girls.

Had I known you'd follow me, I would have been more prepared. I didn't have enough supplies to drug all three of you, so I left for the pharmacy. When I left Jake in my attic, I intended to come back and finish the job. But the thing is, I underestimated you and Chloe. You bitches broke-in my house before I could come back.

I made a mistake; thinking you two weren't as smart as you are. And I've learned from it now. And thanks to you, my mistake forced me to change my ways.

Enough time has gone by that it is now safe for me to get in contact with you to say thanks. I wanted to personally say goodbye and thank you for what you did for me. Ellie, you are the reason I tried something new!

Killing a female wasn't as satisfying as killing a male but, in this case, I was happy to do it. So happy that I think I will do it again! It's enthralling to take advantage of a man. However, I never knew how equally enticing it would be to take advantage of a woman too. I thank you for that, Ellie. You opened up a whole new experience for me!

I hope you have a beautiful rest of your life

with Noah and please tell him to have a safe business trip next month. Make sure he watches his surroundings. You never know how many crazies you'll encounter in New York City. Or is he going to LA this week? Or San Francisco? I might have the days mixed up.

Chloe put up a good fight but, in the end, she couldn't use her self-defense techniques on me. Hell, I do this for a living. She's only killed once. But see, I'm a professional. I've had way more experience than she has. It's kind of funny when you think about it though because I thought Chloe would at least put up a better fight given her history with Jarod.

But she didn't. Killing her was easy.

Thanks to you, Ellie, once I realized that I became your little hobby, I took my time to turn you and Chloe into my hobby too. I know everything about you two.

Excuse me, I know everything about you. I did know everything about Chloe. There's nothing left to know about a person anymore once they are dead.
Rest In Peace, Chloe Jones.

Ellie, you and I will reconnect soon. Until then, I'll be keeping tabs on you just like I know you're looking out for me too.

Love,
Theresa.

THE WOMAN I BEFRIENDED

ACKNOWLEDGEMENTS

My husband; Enrique

My father; Matt

My uncles; Joey & Chris

& special thanks to all the indie authors and readers
who support me.
To anyone I reached out to in the process of creating
this book; to anyone who gave their input in making
this story happen, I will forever be grateful.

A b o u t   t h e   A u t h o r

Sara Kate started her writing career as a scriptwriter for promotional videos and short films. Years later, she wrote her first mystery novel and continues to write full-time in her RV. Aside from writing, she enjoys rollerblading, photography, painting, and anything thriller/mystery related.

INSTAGRAM.COM/SARAKATEAUTHOR

FACEBOOK.COM/SARAKATEAUTHOR

GOODREADS.COM/SARAKATEAUTHOR

BOOKBUB.COM/SARAKATEAUTHOR

PINTEREST.COM/SARAKATEAUTHOR/S

ARA-KATES-BOOKS

SARAKATEAUTHOR.COM

Chapter 1

June 1st

12:22 a.m.

I'm supposed to be the only person in my apartment, but I know my dog did not say bless you to me after I just sneezed.

I get up from my couch in the living room with my bowl of soup when someone knocks on my front door. My dog barks, startling me. The bowl falls right out of my hands and onto the floor. "Thanks, Lola," I say as I pick her up and carry her to the window beside my door.

It's almost half an hour past midnight and I'm not expecting any company. Then again, I don't expect anyone to knock during the day either.-I don't see anyone in the hallway when looking through the window behind my curtain, but there is a brown paper bag by my doorstep. It's from *Wing Central,* which is a restaurant that I often get delivered. One of my neighbors must have typed the wrong apartment number in an online order though, because I didn't order from there tonight. The delivery person is gone, and none of my neighbors are outside, so I guess the food is mine now. Perfect timing, since the knock inadvertently caused me to spill the last of what was in my fridge, anyway.

After setting the bag on my kitchen counter, I pull out three to-go containers; twelve buffalo wings, calamari, and fries. Before eating, I post a photo of my plate on my social media profile with the caption: Food tastes better when it's free! A black heart and fire emoji.

Minutes later, as I'm eating, Lola barks at another knock and I nearly drop my food again. After six years of having her, I know that she's going to bark every time someone knocks on my door, yet it still startles me.

When peeking through the window behind my curtain, I see a woman walking away from my apartment toward the stairs, so I go outside.

"Excuse me? I didn't order this," I call out to her as I pick up another takeout bag. This one is from *5ᵗʰ Liquors*. She walks back over to me, looks up at the number next to my door above my mailbox, then back at the receipt on the bag, and shrugs. "The address says Apartment 7. It's already paid for."

I bring the bag inside and pull a bottle of wine only halfway out of the bag. It's enough to see the label, *Pinot Noir,* and it's the expensive kind too. *Free food and now free wine in one night?* Yeah, somebody must have ordered to the wrong address because nobody would send me this on purpose.

About four hours later, when I am sleeping, Lola abruptly wakes me up by barking. Half-asleep, I sit up and reach over to turn on the lamp that's on top of my nightstand. She's sniffing and scratching the purple carpet under my door. I stumble out of bed, thinking she needs to go out. When I open the door, she immediately races down the hallway, and my eyes follow where she's heading.

She's running straight toward my front door, my front door that's slightly left open, not unlocked… open. I *did not* leave it that way before going to bed.

Panicking, I rush over to shut the door and a strong whiff of cologne hits me once I turn the lock. *Did someone just leave or are they still here?*

I turn around to look in my living room and kitchen. Nobody is in either room, but someone could be in the spare bedroom or my bathroom. I ran right past both doors in the hallway once I saw Lola head toward the living room.

I need to call the police and my cellphones in my bedroom, past those two doors. I need a weapon first.

My mace… I need my keys. Wait, where is my purse? It's not hanging next to my front door like I normally leave it. My eyes shift to the living room, where I spot my black purse sitting on top of my coffee table instead.

With the mace tightly clasped in my hand now, I head toward the hallway to get to my bedroom. I stop briefly in front of the bathroom on my right. Quickly, I flip the light switch on the wall with one hand while my other hand is still gripping the mace, but no one is inside. *I smell cologne again, though.* The back door is still locked. I strung the chain across the top, right before I went to bed.

I rush across the hallway and into the spare bedroom. Then I flip on the light switch.

Slight relief sets over me because nobody is here. I only see the bags of clothes that my best friend left me before she moved out a few months ago. The closet doors are still open like normal, and my paintings are on the floor like they should be.

I don't smell any cologne in here either.

I hurry into my bedroom to get my cellphone off the nightstand. When I walk back out, Lola is sniffing every inch of the floor, from the living room to the kitchen. She only does that after somebody, other than myself, has been in my apartment. She sniffs the person's trail of where they walked after they leave. Now she's heading toward the bathroom.

As I frantically call 9-1-1 on my cell, the

wine bottle on the kitchen counter catches my eye. *Why is it sitting outside of the bag?* I left it *inside* of the bag, not next to the bag. I remember that because I didn't even pull the wine out all the way.

I examine my apartment while waiting for an operator to answer the phone. Nothing seems to be stolen or out of place.
Except for the wine bottle… and maybe my purse.

If you enjoyed this book, please leave a review on Amazon and Barnes & Noble!